24

L.L. Press
Texas

Melissa Hailey

"A harmless man is not a good man. A good man is a very dangerous man who has that under voluntary control."

-Jordan Peterson

Table of Contents

Chapter 1: Shot to the Heart

Rigo examined his gore-covered hands. His eyes followed the red trail over to the blood puddling on the sidewalk. He could hear it dripping into the storm drain. The metallic smell of fear permeated the air of this café terrace in Gatineau, formerly called Hull, Québec, which had just been the scene of a blizzard of gunfire.

Davic's body was obscured by medical personnel. Had he imagined there were still life signs when the medics arrived?

Rigo clearly remembered Davic losing consciousness. The blue eyes rolling up into his head. Is that when Davic had died, the gurgled breathing just death rattles? Had Rigo just felt his own heart when he felt for a pulse? He had never seen so much blood. The amount seemed impossible to come from just one man, but no one else had been hit.

"Can you tell us what happened?" asked a Royal Canadian Mounted Police officer, jolting Rigo back to reality. He had to pause a moment.

How had all this happened?

Davic had found the café and his new boss, Rigo, without issue. Sure enough, the first thing out of Rigo's mouth was the one thing Davic hated most of all: the way he called him "D." Rigo looked up from the sports section of *The Ottawa Sun* as he approached and smiled.

"Hey D, you made it finally."

"My name is not D," he said through a tight jaw. "My name is Davic, kind of like David but not." The ire clear in his raised voice, Davic's light blue eyes burned like a natural gas flame in anger. "In fact you should just be calling me Mr. Woods."

Davic had made this point politely in the past. This was

an intentional slight, Davic thought as the acid in his stomach churned, giving him heartburn.

The meeting with the representatives from Québec had been aggravating. His willpower was waning, his inner savage animal on the verge of being unleashed.

Davic contemplated leaving after that outburst. All eyes were now on them, including pedestrians who had stopped in their tracks as he sniped back at his boss. He refused to let Rigo win at any rate. Davic's rational mind eased him back to his placid demeanor. Rigo simply looked across the table at him with that smug smile, like a cat that had just gotten away with eating the family canary.

"Are you finished playing the martyr or would you like to spend some more time on the cross, Mr. Woods?" Rigo snapped back.

Davic picked the menu back up and grumbled a half-hearted apology to him.

"Looks like the Senators got the third seed in the playoffs," Rigo said as the waiter brought a large plate of sushi and sashimi for the table. Between mouthfuls of raw tuna and salmon dipped in the wasabi-mixed soy sauce in a tiny bowl on the side, Rigo told Davic to contact the team and see if a luxury box would be available at the next game.

Sports were never something Davic found interesting. To him they had very little real-world impact, just a pastime for those who were not competent enough to be productive. Davic always hated when he was relegated to babysitter for the husband of the most powerful woman in North America, arguably the world. Fortunately this had only been an occasional duty in his job as Jordan Innis's senior adviser, aide, whatever other term you could think of, in essence her unelected second-in-command.

He ordered the rest of his lunch and as they waited, he pulled out files from his shoulder bag and put them in order. He handed them over to Rigo.

"Here are charity events coming up that would be nice if you could attend in the role as the Canadian Prime Minister's husband," he said.

Davic went back to reading his notes on Parliamentary issues on his BlackBerry. Davic flicked his eyes up to see Rigo grinning at him. He knew Rigo was intent to get another rise out of him. He ignored him.

Unknown to the two men, their every move was being watched through binoculars from two streets over, through an alleyway. On the other side of the lenses, the man grinned as the plan was put into motion: The van parked in position outside the restaurant, 50 feet down from the terrace.

He watched his men check their guns one last time. Once these bullets were inside the body, they would fragment and slice up the vital organs.

The interloper would no longer be pulling the strings at 24 Sussex.

The difference between a freedom fighter and terrorist was a matter of who won or lost. A man beside the observer nudged him with an elbow, letting him know the gunmen were ready.

Davic heard the screams of other patrons as the masked men rushed onto the restaurant terrace, their weapons brazenly displayed. He slammed Rigo to the ground and knocked the breath out of him. Rigo was stunned - when had the BlackBerry addict Davic become so strong? One of the masked men pulled Davic off of Rigo. Davic stood, his eyes looking down the assault rifle. A sweat had already broken out over Davic's forehead, his thin limbs trembling in fear as the weapon hypnotically held Davic's attention.

Rigo was pulled up to his feet, a gun to his head.

"Mr. *Innis,*" said a male voice.

Jordan Innis, Canada's Prime Minister, had refused to take his last name when they married, so often he was addressed by her last name, to his consternation.

But this was no mistake. The fury in the voice could only have been trumped by the fury from the man's gun.

They put a hood over Rigo's head and zip-tied his hands in front of him. Rigo's resistance was met with a Taser. He felt the electricity run through his body, all his muscles cramping, as he lost consciousness. They dragged Rigo toward the van.

"Monsieur Woods," said the leader of the masked men, the gun still in Davic's face. "Want to join your American cousin or the dead?"

Davic, thin and frail-looking, had not lashed out at the masked men, and they had expected that. Maybe he liked the humiliation. Or perhaps he was secretly thankful - now Jordan would be his for the taking.

Instead of answering, Davic grabbed the gun muzzle and pulled the leader toward himself. He hit the masked man's head with his phone and the blow sent the man crumpling to the ground followed by the shards of what had been Davic's beloved device. Davic scanned the area, where he saw people huddled under their tables, or running for safety. Then he saw the men dragging Rigo to a van parked at the curbside.

Davic ran after them. The abductor with the Taser tried to pistol-whip Davic, but the blow missed the mark. He tossed it aside to grab a gun from his waist, but Davic's hard shoulder threw him onto the pavement with a crack. Without missing a beat, Davic launched himself at the man still trying to haul Rigo into the van.

What should have been a well-rehearsed, nearly foolproof plan to abduct the Prime Minister's American spouse had somehow become a quagmire. Never in any of their run-throughs of the plan did they ever think the stick figure, Woods, would try to resist. The worst they expected was Davic to run away and they would have to shoot him in the back of the head.

Rigo was jolted back to consciousness when he was

dropped to the ground. His ears were ringing with the sound of fists hitting flesh and bone, and the grunts of pain and exertion. He managed to pull off the hood from his head and quickly got his bearings.

After dropping Rigo, the third abductor turned to face Davic and automatically unleashed a flurry of bullets, each shot a dim echo to Rigo's ears. Davic's shirt was torn apart and blood spewed out before he fell heavily backward.

The adbuctor who had had the Taser was quickly to his feet and raced for the van as his accomplice fired up the engine. The van peeled away, leaving Rigo crawling toward Davic.

Davic, writhing on the street, flinched when he saw Rigo's face over his. The Prime Minister's husband's eyes were wide, but at least he was safe - Jordan would be happy about that.

The pain was consuming Davic. He turned to the group gathered in front of the restaurant.

"Is everyone OK?" he asked Rigo.

Blood was pouring from the wounds. Davic pulled at his tie to loosen it. His chest heaved, he coughed up blood. Davic moved his hands along his front, investigating where the blood was coming from.

Rigo tried to place pressure on Davic's wounds but there were too many.

"Rigo, you need to tell Jor, I..."

A coughing fit put him on his side.

More people joined the group in front of the restaurant after crawling out from their hiding places. It had happened so quickly, they hadn't been sure what was going on. As a stunned silence engulfed what had once been a café, some of the patrons pulled out their cell phones and with shaking hands dialed 911.

"...brave," Davic whispered.

Was this what his father experienced before he had died? He had always hoped that between exsanguination and freezing, his father had just fallen asleep and slipped away. Those were things he told himself to comfort his conscience.

Out of habit Davic's hands patted his pants pockets, searching for his BlackBerry. He mumbled some more, his eyes closing.

"Davic, come on, stay with me, buddy!" Rigo cried.

Davic twitched slightly. The man whom Davic had knocked out with his BlackBerry was groaning and trying to get up on the terrace.

Davic's heart, which had been racing just a few moments ago, began to slow down as Rigo heard the sirens come racing down the street. It seemed like an eternity for the paramedics and RCMP to finally arrive on scene, as if the entire world had suddenly flipped to slow motion. Every time Davic's breathing paused, Rigo willed him to inhale again, for his heart to pump once more.

Meanwhile, Nigella, British Prime Minister Basil Thatcher's daughter, smiled as she took in lungs full of the fresh Canadian air. She was giddy. Davic had no clue she was going to be working in the High Commission in Ottawa.

She had thoughts of them getting serious and living together. She would prefer to stay in 24 Sussex and see how it compared to 10 Downing Street. She did not know how big his room was and if it could accommodate her and her hat collection. Alternatively they could get a flat. She felt jittery at the thought that he was close by and shortly she would have her Agent Q in her arms and they would start their happily ever after.

"This is so exciting," she squealed, squeezing Smyth's arm.

Smyth nodded, "Just wait to see the look on his face when he comes into his office and sees you."

He was here officially to set up security details for

Nigella, diplomatic passport and all. Unofficially, he was here to make sure Nigella, dubbed "the British Tart" by tabloids, would not further embarrass her father's administration.

Nigella had noted Davic was moody of late, probably due to the lack of leader summits in the near future where they could be together.

Nigella's excitement was infectious. Smyth found himself smiling. The Boy was going to get the wife and kids he had wanted, the happy and full life Smyth had promised him.

They arrived at 24 Sussex without fanfare. Captain Morgan Remy, head of the Parliamentary Protective Service, had known they were coming. He escorted Smyth and Nigella to Davic's office to wait for him. They had about half an hour before they expected him. Davic would be expecting a meeting with the High Commission's liaison officer.

Nigella, still on an emotional high, sat in Davic's chair and spun around. She stopped, noticing her picture on his desk.

"Oh, he loves me, see," she said, showing Smyth the photo.

Smyth just nodded. She was grinning when she caught her reflection in the computer monitor.

The smile dropped from her face. "Oh my god, I look terrible. He can't see me like this. He'd go running for the hills."

She was shown to a bathroom to freshen up.

Smyth knew she could be a while. She still could be childish. She had matured since she and Davic had started dating. He often wondered if Davic saw in her the childhood he never had. It had never made sense to Smyth why Davic would choose her but that was love. In any case it allowed Smyth access to Davic's life.

Suddenly Smyth's attention was drawn to a commotion

downstairs. He quietly went down and saw Rigo, bloodstained, enter the foyer along with two PPS officers.

Jordan and Captain Remy were in the Prime Minister's study talking in heated tones; the events out on the terrace had already reached them before Rigo arrived at 24 Sussex.

"How could this happen, *where were your men?*" she demanded.

Remy paused, his professional military tone hiding the stress in his voice.

"He was shot at least three times. He's in emergency. I'll update you as soon as I know more. I don't have a next-of-kin listed for him. You are his emergency contact."

Rigo entered his wife's office, still dazed. Jordan ran to him, flinging her arms around him. She pulled away to look him over to make sure he was in one piece. She felt something damp on her white blouse. She looked down and saw deep red.

Smyth wandered in behind. He looked despondent. Rigo gave him a confused look.

"We were here to surprise Davic," Smyth said. "Me and Nigella. What happened? Where is he?"

"We were ambushed, he was shot," Rigo stuttered. "They have a man in custody - extremists. Davic, I don't know if he's gonna make it."

Rigo bowed his head, eyes welling up with the reality of his words.

"Has Cy been called?" Smyth said, pulling out his phone. "I have his number."

Smyth dialed his phone. "Cy, are you sitting?" he asked. "I have some bad news about Davic."

"What's going on?" Nigella asked, peeking through the door of the study.

Jordan and Rigo stared at her blankly.

"Bloody hell, what happened to you?" Nigella said to Rigo.

"What hospital did they take him to?" Smyth asked, realizing he had not gotten that bit of information.

"Davic was shot," Jordan said.

"Don't take the piss out of me," Nigella said hesitantly.

"Cy, get someone to drive you," Smyth said over the phone. "I'll send you the details when I know more. Please keep me updated on the Boy."

He hung up.

Tears were running down Nigella's cheeks, causing her mascara to run. Smyth put his arms around her and rocked her. She became a quivering mass, crying and hyperventilating. Smyth could not help but cry as well.

Chapter 2: Christmas

The Christmas tree lights twinkled as instrumental Christmas music played softly in the background. Six-year-old Davic had fallen asleep by the wood stove, a book about mechanics for children hugged to his chest. His grandmother draped his security blanket over him, smiling.

She went back to work arranging the "To Davic from Santa" gifts them under the tree. She couldn't wait to see his face when he opened the bike. On a recliner slept Davic's father, James, snoring slightly. On his chest was Davic's little sister, Evelyn. This would be her second Christmas but she was still not at the stage where she could open her own gifts or understand what was going on.

Davic's grandfather entered from the cold farmyard.

"I need to get a picture of this," he said.

He fumbled for his camera over the fireplace. He heard the front door open, the freezing wind outside howl, glass shattered, and a new arrival cursed.

Veronica stumbled into the room, drunk, and ripped Evelyn off of James. Evelyn wakened with a start and started wailing.

James burst upright, dizzy.

"What the hell—"

"Shut up. She's *my* kid, the *freak show*'s yours," she said, gesturing to Davic, who now sat up, clutching his book like a stuffed animal.

"Give her back to me," James ordered. "I'll put her back to bed."

"She needs her mother," Veronica snarled.

"You're drunk. She doesn't need that," James insisted.

Veronica cursed and handled the child roughly again.

Veronica's sloppy coordination made it easy for James to take the infant back. He rocked the child, getting her to calm back down.

"Daddy, what's going on?" Davic asked, now at his father's foot.

"Sometimes adults get mad when they drink too many adult drinks," James said.

James headed upstairs with Evelyn. Davic remained staring at his angry mother. She reached out to grab him by the collar. Davic jumped out of her reach, knowing she would yell at him. He screamed, dropping his blanket and book. He ran off, hiding under the Christmas tree.

Veronica's father furiously grabbed the slight-framed woman and pushed her down on the couch before she chased her son. He stood over her a moment before his expression softened, his eyes filling up.

"Veronica, we've all had enough of this, all right? It's about time you started behaving like a *real* mother, stop terrorizing your son."

"Don't tell me how to parent," Veronica hissed. "He's *my* son!"

"Then where were you until he turned four?" her father growled. "So help me, God."

"What? *What*, you old fuck?"

"Veronica," her mother started quietly. "Listen to me: We've talked with James. If you don't go somewhere to get sober, he's gonna sue for full custody of both kids. And your father and I will testify on his behalf."

James came back downstairs, started looking for Davic, and Veronica snarled at him before looking back at her mother.

"You *bitch*," she spat at her mother.

James looked at the confrontation.

"You're trying to steal my children?"

"No, sweetie—"

"We're trying to *protect* them from you," Veronica's

father said.

"You've always hated me, you miserable fucks."

"Get out of this house," her father said.

Veronica had no problem obliging. She turned and staggered down the hallway toward the front door, snatching the keys to James' company car out of a ceramic cup.

"Veronica, you can't drive," James started after her.

"Get the fuck away from me!"

She pulled open the door and rushed out into the snow but was tackled by James, both sinking into the snow. James wrestled the keys out of her hand, then left her in the snow as he stood and turned back toward the house.

Davic stood in the doorway.

"Daddy, look out!"

James only got a quick glance before he dove for a snowbank and missed the clumsy ax swing. Davic went running toward his father. James was to his knees when Davic took a running leap, locking his arms around his father's neck, pressing his tear-stained cheek to his father's chest. James turned his back to his homicidal wife and tensed, waiting for the ax blow to strike.

But instead Veronica screamed. It was not a scream of anger but of pain. James glanced back and saw Veronica kneeling in the snow, the ax sticking out of her foot.

"Go back inside," James told his son.

"No," cried Davic.

Veronica's parents had rushed outside at Davic's warning to his father. Now James and them whispered. Davic went to his mother and put her head in his lap. He stroked her hair and sang her a lullaby, one he often sung to his little sister.

"I don't know if there's ambulance service this far out," Grandpa told James. "Even if there is, they may be off over Christmas."

James resolved he would have to drive Veronica to the

hospital. Veronica's parents did what they could to slow the bleeding in their daughter's foot. Davic insisted he was coming with them to the hospital. James knew he would have to bring Davic with him, lest he have a panic attack.

With Davic in the car, James returned to the house to help Veronica to the car, but she pulled away.

"Get Evelyn," she demanded.

"No, she's staying—" James began.

"I'm *not* leaving her with these deceitful people!" Veronica said, glancing over at her parents. "Get my daughter or I'll bleed to death right here!"

Veronica's father was on the verge of exploding, but James soothed him quietly, then headed upstairs to get Evelyn and her things.

"Davic, you sure you don't want to stay with us?" Grandma asked as James buckled Evelyn into her carseat.

Davic nodded, kissed and hugged his grandparents.

"You can open *your* presents from Santa but please leave mine till we get back," he told them as he buckled himself into his car seat. "I wanna make more cookies with Grandma too."

Veronica passed out before the car made it to the end of the long farm driveway. It was a three-hour drive to the closest town with a hospital.

"So I was reading about airfoils," Davic said from his carseat diagonally across from James' seat. "They're how planes fly, the wings. What's the lift formula?"

"You mean Newton's Second Law?" James asked

"Yeah."

James explained. He had read technical books to Davic as a baby. As he got older Davic still wanted his father to read books about mechanical and computer engineering to him. James thought Davic just wanted to hear his voice. But eventually James realized Davic had been absorbing what he was reading to him.

Veronica had abandoned them when Davic was only

four months old. James had cut a business trip short as he had not been able to get hold of Veronica. The nanny he had hired while he was gone had been turned away. In his gut he knew something was not right.

He entered the house calling for Veronica, but the house was quiet and still. She could have been out - the car was missing. He went to their bedroom and found the dresser drawers strewn across the room, empty. He hurried across the hallway to Davic's nursery. When he entered, the smell repelled him like an electric fence.

Veronica had let dirty diapers pile up around the room and these had attracted flies, roaches, and the trapped air in the room was like acid to his lungs. Still, James ran to the crib and saw the tiny emaciated baby covered in shit. James struggled not to pull his son too frantically out of the crib. Davic's diaper fell off of its own weight. He hurried Davic out into the living room, not knowing what to do but cradle him and cry. He sat on the floor, rocking and crying. He grabbed a throw blanket and wrapped his son, then examined the tiny form: Davic opened his pale blue eyes and locked onto his father, blinking a few times.

He called the ambulance from his landline. Davic opened his eyes again as the medic jabbed him repeatedly with an IV needle in his foot. He was so weak, he hardly resisted the multiple attempts to find a vein. Any normal child would have been screaming bloody murder.

After the IV was in, the medics fretted over his heart rate. Davic's little body seemed lost in the vast expanse of a stretcher designed an adult. They did not have the specialized equipment for infants. The adult oxygen mask obscured his whole face.

James held his little hand during the ride to the hospital. He could see the dark judging looks from the medics. It was not important to explain to strangers. James held to the fact Davic was moving more. He had always been an active baby, smiling at everyone and cooing, as though trying to add his thoughts to the conversation. Seeing Davic so still was bizarre.

He never let Davic out of his sight at the hospital. The X-rays and other diagnostic tests ruled out any other cause besides neglect. Davic had been starving and extremely dehydrated. James sat beside Davic's bed in a critical pediatric ward.

James was not left alone with Davic for any significant period – a nurse was stationed outside the room.

But all that mattered to him was Davic's eyes were open and he was looking at his father, cooing. James talked to him about the first boring topic to pop into his mind: how to program a simple database search program. That's when the police officer entered the room.

"You James Woods?" the officer asked.

"Yes," James replied, not looking up from Davic.

"Detective Irwin. I'd like to have a little chat. Best if we do it down at the station."

"Can this wait?"

"This concerns your son and your wife. If we can clear this up now, you can avoid child protective services."

It was a subtle, passive threat but James recognized it.

"I guess I don't really have a choice if I want to keep my son."

He gave Davic a kiss on the head and as James followed the officer out, he heard Davic fussing.

"You said you were on a business trip," Detective Irwin said once he and James were seated in the interrogation room, which was just a jail cell with cement-block walls in place of steel bars. "I need details, locations, contacts."

"I can't discuss that. You can get a hold of CSIS to confirm my whereabouts," James said, jittery from the coffee.

CSIS was the Canadian Security Intelligence Service. "You work for CSIS?" asked the detective.

James shook his head "No, contractor."

He paused.

"If that's all, I'd like to get back to my son."

"We are gonna have to hold you on child endangerment till your story checks out," the officer said, opening the interrogation room door and motioning for James to head out first.

It took a day but CSIS was able to confirm that James was "elsewhere" and the nanny James had hired, and whom Veronica had scared out of the house, verified Davic had been left with only his mother.

They released James, who immediately returned to the hospital. Davic smiled and giggled when he came back into the room.

That night he read technical manuals to Davic. He saw it as multi-tasking: The kid just wanted to hear his voice as he went to sleep and he could read for work at the same time. The nurses still eyed him with suspicion but Davic was eventually discharged into his care.

Davic's first panic attack was when he was three: James left Davic with a sitter and headed for work. The sitter told him later that Davic immediately started crying, wailing, his chest heaving. This went on for so long that he turned blue and she thought he was having a seizure or a heart attack and rushed him to the hospital.

After this happened two more times, James started taking Davic with him to work, where he was fascinated by schematics and watching his dad work.

Growing up, Davic did not know his father worked at one of the highest-security facilities in the world. It's a difficult concept to explain to a toddler, even a smart one. Davic started parroting overheard conversations and started trying to draw the schematics he saw. James' boss, instead of being mad, was impressed by Davic and hired a private teacher to look after the child while James worked.

Life had been good till Veronica came back into their lives. James knew he should have turned her away. He just could not contemplate what would happen to the unborn child she carried. He let her convince him she had changed and she was ready to come back and be a mom. Children with two parents often did better in life and Davic deserved the best chance.

Davic had finally fallen asleep in the car, the book on mechanics still in his hands. James looked at the car clock, noting it was now Christmas morning.

"Merry Christmas," he whispered to all in the car.

A loud sound and a flash of light shook his bones as the car lurched off the road and down an embankment before he had a chance to react. The concussive wave shattered the windows, sending jagged diamonds flying into the air, pelting the occupants.

Once still, something in the metal work of the car was ticking, the engine was burning snow that had gotten under the jack-knifed hood.

"Dad?" Davic whimpered out, a hand reaching out to the driver's seat.

"Are you OK?" James asked in between groans.

"I got a bump on the head. It hurts."

James nodded, his face screwed up in pain "Can you move?"

Davic unbuckled himself and crawled over to Evelyn's car seat behind James. The seat was at an odd angle, broken off its base, and the door had been crushed inward on that side. Small cubes of safety glass filled the car seat.

"Evelyn," Davic said as though trying to wake her up to play with her as he gently shook her.

She should be crying, James thought, if she were alive.

Davic couldn't tell her neck was broken.

"I think she's asleep," Davic said, reaching down for her blanket from the car floor. He wrapped her in it, then gave her a kiss on the forehead.

As Davic did that, James, trying to hold onto his senses and not let himself be overwhelmed with despair, reached out for Veronica. She was slumped in her seat. James had not buckled her in. Her head had broken the passenger-side window. He stroked her hair.

"Veronica?"

When he pressed her shoulder, her head lolled limply to the side. Checking for a pulse, he found none.

He could not let Davic see her like this. Grandma had put a coat over her before they'd left the farm. He covered her head with it.

He was briefly overcome and let out a cry of grief. Davic watched from behind him as he caught his breath. Then James assessed his own predicament: His legs were pinned between the crushed-in door and the center console, trapping him. When he tried to wiggle out, he felt a sharp stabbing in his left side. The realization of the latter seemed to activate the depletion of his strength and to arouse shock waves of pain, which he could only so long stifle himself from venting aloud and frightening his son. He had to get Davic out of here.

"Dav, I need you to crawl up here and find my cell phone."

Davic did as asked and brought the phone up from the floor in between his mother's feet. James saw there was no cell service on this stretch of road.

"Is Mom sleeping too?" Davic asked.

"Yes, don't try to wake her," James said.

"What happened?"

"Must have hit black ice and slipped off the road."

After trying to conjure alternatives but coming up empty, James' throat contracted to try to control his trembling voice before he spoke.

"You need to go get help."

Davic burrowed into his father's coat, putting his ear to his father's heart. His arms were too short to wrap around his father's waist and perhaps graze the wound in James' side - thank God. If Davic saw blood, the panic attack might kill him.

"No. I'm scared."

"Dav, you have to be brave and get in your snowsuit," James said, his voice going high with strain at the end.

Despite his fear, Davic did as told and pulled on his snowsuit. James helped him the best he could. James then pulled a flashlight out of the console and handed it and his cell phone to his son.

"You get up to the road," James said. "If you see a car, you wave them down. Otherwise, when you get a signal on my phone, you dial the numbers 911. When there are bars up in the corner of the screen? That's when you have a signal. You understand?" James asked, the pain somehow getting worse.

"No," whined Davic as he went back to clinging to his father.

James hugged Davic and stroked his back.

"I love you, son. No matter what, I love you."

"I love you too, Daddy."

James' cough brought up blood, which he caught on the back of his hand and quickly wiped on the side of his seat.

"There's so much I wanna to teach you and tell you…"

The pain reached an apex, which he survived by clutching a handful of his jacket, without an ounce more pressure on his son. But then there was a rapid sinking feeling in his gut and his grip on his jacket weakened uncontrollably, numbness spreading.

"Dad?" Davic said.

It took a moment for James to open his eyes and focus. "It's cold...You're cold," Davic said.

James nodded.

Davic crawled back and retrieved his security blanket. He spread it over his father.

"Dav, go to the road," James said in a raspy whisper.

Davic uneasily crawled out the smashed window on what had been his side of the car. He looked at the car wreck, wanting to go back to the safety of his father's arms.

"See you later, alligator," Davic called back.

James didn't respond with the anticipated, "After a while, crocodile." He didn't respond at all.

Davic climbed up the steep embankment. It took some time but he made it to the road again. He started walking along the side, nestling into his snowsuit.

The clock on the phone told him he had been walking for two hours and 46 minutes when a snowplow approached. Davic waved the lit flashlight and the driver stopped and climbed down from the truck.

"What the hell you doin'—"

"My family is stuck, we have to get them out!"

The driver looked over Davic and saw frost had formed on the outside of his snowsuit. He also saw dark stains, which were difficult to identify against the dark material.

"Kid, let's get you outta the cold."

The driver helped Davic up into the heated cab. He told the driver his name and what he could about the accident, remembering the term "black ice," then the driver picked up his radio.

"Dispatch, I have a kid here. Call out EMT - his family was in a car accident. something happened to his family. Over."

"Copy. Calling EMT and giving them your location.

Good luck," dispatch said.

The driver got back into his seat and put the plow in motion again, following the forward tracks Davic had made in the snow along the side of the road.

In the time he'd been walking, Davic's mind had run wild with the possibilities this situation presented, each worse than the last. The walking, though, had also given him an outlet to occupy his energy and not let emotions cripple him. Now, in a state of rest, he was and remained for the majority of the ride on the verge of tears, which the plow driver noticed and awkwardly adjusted himself in his seat. All he could say was that his name was Mack.

Davic was stunned at how short the distance back to the crash site was. When he saw the footsteps trail off from the road shoulder, Mack parked the plow as near to the side as he could.

"Kid, stay here," Mack said as he pulled on his coat and opened his door.

But Davic rushed out even as Mack tried to grab him. Once out, Davic scrambled back down the embankment.

Davic approached the shattered driver's-side door window.

"Daddy…"

He paused, waiting for his father to reply. Ice had formed on James' eyelashes. His skin had always been pale; now it was nearly the same color as the snow. James had pulled Davic's security blanket up to the side of his head to use as a pillow.

As Davic started to cry, two Mounties came down the embankment. One came up beside Davic, the other came upon the passenger side of the car. This officer checked on Veronica while the first removed his glove and put his fingers to James' neck. Once it was confirmed, he checked the back seat and saw Evelyn, who was so frozen, she reflected the moonlight.

An ambulance pulled up to the side of the road, its

flashing lights beaming over the embankment. Two medics came down. One checked the car while the other joined Davic and the Mountie.

"Davic?" the first Mountie said. "I need you to go with this man. He'll take care of you, OK?"

Davic felt the medic's hand drop on his shoulder and he pulled away. The Mountie and the medic tried to soothe him at the same time as they tried to apprehend him and Davic slapped them away.

The second officer came up behind Davic, taking off his jacket and belt, and he flung the jacket over Davic, then cinched it tightly with the belt, an improvised straitjacket. He kicked and yelled as the second officer and the medic carried him up to the ambulance.

The first Mountie searched the dead occupants for ID, then came up to the ambulance, where the medics had affixed an oxygen mask over Davic. On the vitals monitor, his heart rate was over 200.

The Mountie climbed into the ambulance and knelt beside Davic. He produced a white square and showed it to the kid.

"Is this your family?"

Davic's screaming and squirming died down as he looked at the photo. It had been taken about month before for the Christmas cards: his mother, father, sister, and him in front of the Christmas tree.

"If I give you the photo, will you be quiet and still for the medics?" the officer asked

Davic nodded, his attention on the photo as tears rolled down his cheek. The Mountie nodded to the medics, who cautiously unwrapped the restraints. Once free Davic grabbed the photo and held it to his heart.

Chapter 3: My American Boy

Eleven months before Davic and Rigo would be attacked, Quentin sat at his vanity taking off his makeup. His wig sat on a stand beside him.

"Will the Canadians be bringing those handsome Mounties?" he asked, smirking, his other half, the president of the United States.

The handsome, gray-haired man behind him frowned and took a sip of bourbon.

"Don't embarrass me," Beau Delacroix said. "I don't need Jordan Innis to resent me."

"They sure make them good-lookin' up north," the first "lady" said, casting a sidelong look at his husband.

The world, not to mention the United States itself, was not ready for an openly gay couple in the White House. The risks to relationships and negotiations with states that publicly executed gays, or at least where homosexuality was illegal, was too great and would be too devastating to lose.

In public Quentin presented himself as the trophy wife "Queenie." Their private acquaintances knew the truth. But there were rumors, of course, which had so far been dismissed as tin-hat conspiracy theories.

The president rolled his eyes and shook his head. Quentin grabbed a few of the briefing notes.

"Rigoberto Barbossa," he said.

"One of our native sons," Beau said.

"It's always good to have friends who have the ears of world leaders."

"Indeed. Charm him, won't you?"

Quentin smiled.

"How can I resist?"

"*Only* charm."

Quentin stood and put his arms around his husband.

"I hope they don't have sticks up their bums like that decrepit Limey and that tart of a daughter," Quentin said.

"I thought you'd have liked her," Beau said.

"She tried to seduce me - I felt *violated.*"

"You were flirting with her," Beau said.

"I can't help it."

"She'll go after anything shiny with a pulse."

Quentin grinned.

"The PM might be a geezer, but his staff are beautiful," he said. "Wonder if Nigella hired them all from a modeling agency. We should get better looking staff - ours are all fat."

"How would you control yourself?" Beau asked.

Quentin continued looking through the files.

"*Look* at the baby blues on this guy." Quentin said, holding up a photo of Davic. "*Single*, he's been with that redhead since before she took office. Wonder if he likes long walks and Broadway musicals?"

Quentin continued to look through the files, picking out the good-looking men.

"These aren't dating profiles," Beau teased. "Behave yourself and remember: discretion. This isn't New Orleans."

"No, we're in the *sanctum sanctorum*, the White House! I would never *dream* of doing something *untoward* here, Mr. President."

Jordan sat at the head of the conference table, her staff going over their notes about the upcoming trip to the White House.

"Public perception is a tricky one," the PR secretary said. "You can't be too friendly. Rigo and the first lady are a particular concern. We can't have the perception they're using your husband to influence you."

"A lotta people think the wife is just there as window

dressing and that Delacroix is gay," an intern who worked in media monitoring blurted out, to the harsh look of his supervisor.

"I saw the cartoon," Jordan admitted.

It had been caricatures of her, Rigo, and Delacroix in bed together. As a private citizen, Jordan had found it funny.

"I get it," she said. "There can't be any suggestion of a personal relationship, at least not in front of the media."

"On the topic of Rigo," the PR officer went on, "the opposition is accusing him of using his US citizenship to avoid paying Canadian taxes while reaping benefits at the taxpayers' cost. They're gonna use that against us when reelection comes up."

"He's going through the process. Running into a few technical issues. Don't want to be accused of queue jumping." Davic said.

Rigo's most recent application for Canadian citizenship had been rejected because the immigration department had said it had not received his birth certificate. But Davic suspected there was interference slowing the process down. There was nothing he could do to fix it without giving the opposition something to use against Jordan.

Ever since Jordan and Rigo had gotten married, CSIS had repeatedly visited Davic for reports on what Rigo was up to. He'd only reported what he'd seen in passing, he'd never taken any initiative to know more than was obvious. CSIS had implied that if Davic spied and reported on Rigo, they would allow Davic access to his personnel file, which may contain the piece of his life he didn't remember: What had happened between his time as an analyst for CSIS and when he'd been a resident of a rehab center in Victoria, on the other side of the country, recovering from a traumatic brain injury. He'd only been out of the rehab for a day before he'd met Jordan, out on a beach.

When he first asked to review his file, he'd been told it

was classified and only the Prime Minister could request it. Now, even as Jordan's aide, he didn't have the necessary clearance.

It wasn't normal to classify personnel files, especially after the person in question had stopped working for CSIS. He had tried to access the file by hacking into CSIS's servers but the file wasn't digitized.

So far he hadn't indulged their requests. His loyalty to Jordan and her administration's success meant more to him. And with her help, he could access his file anyway. But for now Jordan was too new, the CSIS would delay her request for as long as they could until they could fully vet her background and everyone associated with her. The first step in getting the CSIS to cooperate would be naturalizing Rigo.

"Dav?" Jordan called, bringing Davic out of his thoughts.

"Sorry, where were we?" Davic said, looking at his notes.

"At the end of the agenda. Did you have anything to add?"

"No, I think we have covered it," he said. "The trade agreement is getting all the thumbs up. This is gonna be a productive visit."

The arrival at Andrews Air Force Base went as well as could be expected. An early morning rain passed through and brought with it a sustained wind throughout the day. Jordan's red hair blew wildly as her envoy was officially welcomed to the States by the president and his spouse on the South Lawn of the White House.

Jordan shook the hand of her American counterpart.

"Good to finally meet you. Heard lots about you," she said with the smile plastered on for the cameras of the media gathered on the grass.

"I am impressed with what I have seen so far," Beau

said with a jovial smile. "This must be your husband, Rigo, I have read your articles," Beau said, taking Rigo's hand and giving a hearty shake.

"Pleased to meet you, Mr. President." Rigo said in awe. "I never thought I would actually be doing this, and I can't think of what to say."

Rigo continued in his excitement. Davic cleared his throat and discreetly squeezed Rigo's elbow. Rigo realized he was still hanging on to Delacroix's hand and let go. Davic then guided Rigo out of frame.

As part of the formalities, the two Heads of State walked across the lawn, inspecting the honor guard, before crossing to the other side of the lawn to shake hands with the public that had gathered for the welcoming ceremony.

"I gotta say, she's looking like a natural out there, Rigo, you must be proud of her," Queenie said, effeminately, for Rigo's ears only. He straightened the hem of his dress.

"I am," Rigo said, sighing. "Me, on the other hand, I'm struggling with this...public stuff."

The first lady patted him on the back.

"She'll get you trained yet," he said, laughing.

A few minutes later, the two leaders joined their spouses and entered the White House.

Jordan and Beau entered the Oval Office for the official photo-op for the media. Quentin directed Rigo back toward the stairway to the residence.

"They'll talk shop for about an hour or so," Queenie said as they walked. "Beau was up half the night reviewing his policy positions before he finally gave up and came to bed. What about Jordan? How'd she sleep last night?"

"I passed out before she came to bed," Rigo said. "I don't think she got more than an hour or so."

The clearing throat behind them reminded them that Davic was right behind.

Davic knew Jordan would stay on message without him. Rigo, on the other hand, was the liability that needed to be watched and guided. Davic was glad to get Rigo away from the media, though he'd prefer him not to be with Queenie under any circumstances.

Rigo sighed, as if he were a young student being admonished by his teacher.

"Relax, will you, D? It's not like I'm revealing the secret poutine recipe."

Quentin led them into the East Wing, where traditionally the president's family resided, and in keeping with tradition, the press didn't follow.

Davic took a brief sigh of relief as they entered the residence, now out of range of the media's scrutiny. The opposition would have a field day if a picture or, even worse, a recording were leaked, as Rigo was going beyond the niceties expected - he was coming off completely awe-stuck, hardly the public image Jordan's administration needed projected.

Quentin looked over at Davic and let his eyes wander up and down the tall blond man. He was a bit conservative in his dress but it was still sharp and high end. The fact he had been an aide to a straight female for a long time before she'd met her husband made him think the man must be queer as a three-dollar bill. Of course maybe he and Jordan had, at some point, fraternized but Queenie preferred to think the former.

Davic's light blue eyes were beautiful. He was tall and slender in a kind of boyish way. There was no fat on him but not much muscle either - the body of a teenage boy, no sagging gut. All the blonds he knew started going bald early or their hair went dark. Such was not the case with Davic: He was not an Adonis but it would be fun to have a younger man.

"Is poutine really a Canadian state secret?" Quentin asked, fidgeting with Davic's tie clip.

Davic rolled his eyes.

"Have a seat and tell me about it," Quentin teased,

offering Davic a seat on the sofa.

Davic took it.

"It's more of a French-Canadian thing," Davic said dully, trying to discourage Queenie from engaging him any more.

An attendant entered the room with a tray on which were a pitcher and a half-dozen glasses.

"I hope you both don't mind a little sweet tea," Queenie said, watching the spiked drink being poured and passed around.

"So, tall, blond, and handsome, what's your story?" asked Quentin.

Davic couldn't even wrap his brain around such a broad question. Rigo grinned at Davic's discomfort.

Davic took a long drink, then muttered, "I don't really have much to tell, I'm nobody..."

Then he retreated into his personal haven: his BlackBerry, with which he could occupy himself for hours dealing with various aspects of Jordan's office requiring his attention in order to make life easier for her.

Rigo and Queenie resumed conversation between themselves again and for a little while, Davic was left to himself. Soon, though, as he neared the bottom of his glass, his vision narrowed and was not able to make out the text. His concentration was gone.

He had gone days without sleep before but still had been able to keep his focus. Why was he losing it now?

It took him a moment to determine that the iced tea must be alcoholic - though Davic was not familiar with the taste of normal iced tea or of the various tastes of alcohol. Ever since his brain injury - however he'd sustained it - he had been told not to drink, as it would increase his chances of having a seizure.

To fit into the political world, when he had meetings with politicians in an alcoholic environment, he'd learned to get creative and would usually order a drink with a lot of ice and mixers and with as little alcohol as possible and nurse it the whole night. Other times, he'd tell the bartender that he was the designated driver, and that got him soft drinks for free.

Davic dropped his BlackBerry in his lap irritably. He would just have to wait for his liver to clear the alcohol, then he could get back to work.

An hour later Rigo, Davic, and Queenie heard commotion in the next room over - the dining room.

Davic led the way to join Jordan, Beau, and various other guests gathering at the tables for dinner. Laughter filled the air, reminding Davic more of a rowdy bonfire party than a proper state dinner.

The media had made a spectacle of Jordan and Rigo's arrival at the White House, making it sound like they were attending a celebrity wedding. Jordan had brought some formal gowns, all from Canadian designers. When they'd been out on the lawn, Davic had counted at least a half-dozen "entertainment news" channels that were more popular than most news networks. They had as much understanding of international politics as a dog has with quantum physics.

Instead of reporting on the trade agreement in discussion, or Jordan's record as Prime Minister, these outlets had swooned over her outfit, shouting some of the most inane questions about the name of the designer.

Trying to understand the popularity of these networks made Davic's already pounding head hurt more.

Beau had his arm around Jordan, telling her a dirty joke. The papers stated the relationship was cool and formal - a description straight from Davic's mouth and relayed through a dozen set of ears before spreading to reporters. In truth, the two couples got along great like they had been friends for a long time. But in politics, it was about perception rather than reality.

The Ottawa papers would report her visit to America as Canada imposing its will on a reluctant business partner. However, the truth was everything would be a win-win for both sides. The one thing that still remained, something of a question mark in Davic's mind, was how Rigo was being portrayed. Normally, spouses were invisible, but again, this was America, and Rigo was one of her native sons. Worse, he was one of the media, although the political press looked at sports media with disdain.

Davic's watch over Rigo was compromised since downing the alcoholic iced tea. It became further endangered when champagne was brought out to those gathered at the dining table. While not technically mandatory, Davic could not stand the idea that not drinking it would make Jordan's negotiations with the Americans more difficult, so he drank it. He tried writing a briefing note to himself on his phone but couldn't read what he was typing.

Dinner wound down and the business meeting started.

Beau was finishing a story Queenie had heard a million times, about wrestling a gator, and as usual, Beau embellished. By now, he definitely was riding a buzz from the drinks and that Acadian Bayou accent was in full swing. He was throwing his arms around, reenacting the moves he'd used to get control over the animal, and in doing so knocked a drink into Quentin's lap.

"Beau, this is Versace!" scowled the first lady, the drink instantly staining his dress.

"Oh don't be such a drama queen!" mocked the president.

Quentin excused himself from the table to go change as his husband went back to his story. Shortly after, Beau and Jordan excused themselves to return to the Oval Office to complete their trade talks. Rigo and some of the other attendees were escorted to the Yellow Room, where they were treated to a set by a New Orleans jazz performer.

Quentin soon returned in a new outfit, and sat down next to Rigo.

"OK, darling, now it's time to tell me how you ended up with such a drop-dead gorgeous redhead," Quentin said.

Rigo blushed.

"It's a long story, to be honest, nowhere near as interesting as the tabloids made it out to be after Jordan won."

Quentin patted his leg, "Oh honey, I can sympathize. You know, Beau kept our relationship on the down low at first while he was going after the governorship years ago. I swear, Beau is married to the job more than me, I'm just his mistress...We have an *arrangement*."

Rigo looked sidelong at the first lady, wondering if she were giving him a not-so-subtle hint. Luckily for him, Queenie quickly elaborated.

"That tall blond fellow from earlier...Can you properly introduce us?"

Rigo was amused now. He'd never known Davic to be interested in any woman - or man for that matter - and had come to think he was gay. Or maybe he had no sexual desire at all? He was definitely a workaholic, so maybe his job gave him all the satisfaction he needed.

"That's Davic Woods, Jordan's assistant, my...*babysitter*."

"Can he be trusted?" asked Quentin

"When it comes to Jordan, he'll take whatever is needed to the grave," Rigo smiled, not exaggerating in the least.

In the beginning Davic's devotion to Jordan had concerned Rigo but gradually Rigo had come to see Davic as Jordan did: as a brother - or at the least a stepbrother he didn't hate.

Davic was just then slumped in his seat, facing the jazz player but almost too drunk to listen. Queenie saw his posture and also his opportunity to strike.

Rigo watched with interest as Quentin chatted up Davic after the performance, plying him with more drinks on a couch in the corner of the Yellow Room.

"...the downside was I ended up as the only one at Mardi Gras without any beads," Queenie finished up a story Davic hadn't caught a word of. "I still get up to fun, just can't do it publicly. You're quiet, Davic."

Queenie ran a finger down Davic's chest and Davic blushed, taking another drink.

"I'm just not user-friendly," Davic chuckled.

"What happens when you give a politician Viagra?" Quentin asked.

Davic shrugged.

"They *grow!*"

They both howled with laughter.

"Hurry up and finish that drink," Queenie ordered. "I wanna get you something special."

There was a grin on Davic's face as he came up with a joke to answer Queenie's.

"The NSA: a government organization that actually listens to you!" Davic said before downing the last of his drink.

Rigo had never seen Davic drunk before. He was cursing and driven to tell dirty jokes by the first lady. Who knew the tech-geek-turned-political-aide knew *any* dirty jokes.

Rigo had to admit, at least to himself but never to Davic, that his respect for his wife's most trusted aide was growing. A California senator took Rigo's focus from Davic while querying him on his thoughts on the latest attempt to return the Chargers to San Diego.

Then Davic was telling Queenie stories about his foster father, Mr. Drew, and the trouble he got into at school.

"They were always suspending me for 'conduct unbecoming of a student," he heard Davic boast in a slurred British accent. "This one kid, Mark, took a liking to beating the shit out of me and stealing my lunch. So one day I filled my chocolate pudding with laxative. We called him Skid Mark for the rest of the year."

When Queenie brought him another drink, finally a sober thought crossed Davic's mind.

"I think I've had enough for tonight," he protested tactfully.

"Nonsense, *dear* Davic," Quentin insisted. "You wouldn't want to offend your hosts now, would you?"

His lilting Louisiana accent, with a Southern twang mingled with a soupçon of traditional Acadian French undertones, mesmerized Davic into accepting the libation.

Quentin was happy with how Davic was reacting: The first lady had his hand unopposed on Davic's knee and had been working up his thigh. Davic was smiling at him.

"Davic, why don't I give you a personal tour?" Queenie offered, popping up. "Not many know of all the debauchery that's gone on between these walls."

Quentin grasped Davic's arm to stop him from stumbling off in the wrong direction.

This was not Queenie's first foray in using alcohol to get what he wanted. In fact, he'd come to think of himself as something of an liquor chemist, adept at creating cocktails just strong enough to paralyze inhibitions, not to endanger safety. But now he started to think he'd overdone it with Davic. He'd overestimated Davic's tolerance simply because he was Jordan's aide.

No matter. Queenie had a concoction for just such an occasion.

He sat Davic down on the sofa in the residence, then shooed away the Secret Service officers, who reluctantly left the room.

"Mind if I take off my shit – um...shirt? It's getting warm in here," Davic said.

Quentin giggled.

"Oh, you don't know how long I've been waiting for

you to do that."

Quentin went off to the kitchen to combine energy drinks with the addition of several pills from a plastic box he got out of his purse. This would perk Davic back up and make him last all night. Quentin came back out to admire the shirtless Davic. He looked hairless. Whether he really was or his blond hair was just hard to see at this distance, Quentin would find out shortly.

He gave Davic the drink, insisting he taste it. Davic did. Quentin sat down beside Davic, leaning into his body.

"Mind if I take off my shirt too?" Quentin said

"Sure," Davic said, taking another long drink.

"Let me dab the sweat off of you." Quentin suggested.

Davic looked at the now shirtless Quentin and the mass of hair on his chest. Davic just nodded and smiled. Quentin, seeing no adverse reaction, removed the silk-handkerchief from around his neck and wiped Davic's forehead, neck, then down his chest.

Davic laid back his head and closed his eyes. After a moment Quentin started slipping out of his dress.

"Let me give you a back rub," Queenie said.

Davic had no willpower to resist. Queenie pushed him around so he was sitting on the sofa with his back to the first lady, who curled up to his quarry, knowing the hurdles had now been overcome and it was going to be a fun night.

After Davic's shoulders relaxed and became like jelly under his hands, Quentin kissed the nape of Davic's neck and Davic straightened up.

"How do you like it?" Quentin asked in a seductive tone.

There was no reply. Davic just sat there ramrod straight. Queenie worked his way around to a kiss on Davic's lips. The lack of reaction bothered Quentin.

He looked into Davic's eyes. His pupils were almost as wide as his irises and he was staring far away. His body started trembling as he fought to get to his feet, his limbs shaking.

"Davic Woods, technical analyst, CSIS!" Davic yelled, stumbling and knocking over an end table.

"I need help!" Quentin called, beckoning the Secret Service.

The agents burst in. Davic had climbed onto a bookcase but jumped off as it fell forward and he stumbled into another piece of furniture.

Davic seemed unaware of the men approaching. When they came within reach, he flung his arms madly.

"Davic Woods, technical analyst, CSIS!" he repeated in choppy segments

His elbow caught one of the men in the gut, a punch to the jaw for another. That was enough and they decked him to the ground among the shattered remains of the glass decorations that had sat on the bookcase.

One agent kneeled on Davic's back as two others fought with his arms to get them behind him. A fourth held his legs to stop him from kicking. His body bucked and writhed.

Suddenly Davic's fighting changed, all the agents felt it. Instead of trying to resist them, his body was pulsating, as though he were being Tased. The agents released him and backed away. Davic made no attempt to get up, his limbs just shook and jerked.

"I think it's a seizure," said one agent.

They turned him over: Davic's eyes were open but had rolled back, so all that could be seen was the whites.

The door to the residence opened and President Delacroix stood in the doorway.

"What the hell's going on?" he demanded, looking at the overturned furniture and broken glass.

His mind quickly filled the blanks as he recognized Davic lying on his floor, the shaking subsiding.

He could see the headlines: *Canadian PM Aide Dies in Suspected Drug Overdose at the White House.*

"Get the goddamn doctor," Beau ordered and one agent bustled out while the president went to another agent who had his fingers on Davic's neck.

"His heart's racing," the agent said.

"Put him in the spare room."

The agent pulled Davic into his arms and took him into another room. He wanted to throttle Queenie but when Beau looked at him, the lack of color in his spouse's cheeks told him the first lady had suffered enough with the fright.

Queenie told him the story in full.

"Oh Jesus Christ, the Stud Rider, Queenie?"

This was not the first time Quentin had brought back "a toy" to enjoy, but this was the first time he had tried since they'd moved into the White House and the first time something had gone wrong. Considering the ingredients in Queenie's special drink - Red Bull, Viagra, and amphetamines - Beau supposed it was only a matter of time.

Beau went to one agent standing beside the closed door leading into the dining room, out of earshot of the others.

"Call Bowser at the Company," Beau muttered. "Have him bring me this kid's background check."

The agent nodded before leaving.

"We keep this in-house all the way," Beau said loudly to the rest in the room. "We don't tell the Canadians."

He went back beside Queenie.

"Does he know you're a man?" Beau whispered.

"I think so," Quentin said, cowering

Beau shook his head.

"On the bright side, if his heart explodes, we might be back in Baton Rouge in time for Mardi Gras."

The next morning the knock from Davic did not come on Jordan's door. She and Rigo had left separately - Rigo after Davic had disappeared with Queenie.

Jordan repeatedly checked her BlackBerry as she got

dressed.

"I think he had a little too much to drink last night," Rigo said in response to what he saw was worrying her.

"When you see him, I need to have a talk with him," she said as she left for another round of trade talks.

She read the changes to the agreement she and Beau had worked out the previous night as she made her way to the Oval Office.

The new draft was acceptable. The agreement would be drafted up and signed tomorrow.

She wished Davic were here to go over it and find something she was sure she had missed. His absence was startling.

Was he starting to burn out? She added a mental note to figure out a time when he could go on holiday.

She knew she could not lose him, not yet at any rate. She still felt she was an imposter in the Prime Minister's clothing. Without him someone, likely the opposition, would figure that out. Where was he?

She was escorted into the office by two Secret Service officers and Beau was sitting behind his desk, on the phone, which he put down once Jordan entered. She saw he looked upset and took a moment to compose himself. Once the door was closed, he spoke.

"There was an incident last night and I would like to deeply apologize for it, on behalf of my spouse."

Jordan looked confused.

"I'm sorry, Mr. President, I don't know what you're talking about."

Beau breathed a sigh of relief - at least his orders not to leak this to the Canadians had been obeyed.

"Queenie was a little too much of a good host and your Mr. Woods ended up passing out. We're not sure what happened but the staff physician has assured us he'll be just fine."

Jordan felt uneasy. This was another novice mistake, something that would only happen to an imposter unable to control her staff.

"I must apologize, Beau, I hope he wasn't any trouble."

"Let's call this an honest little slip on Queenie's hosting and leave it at that," Beau suggested and Jordan agreed.

Later that day a very hoarse Davic phoned Jordan to apologize and to say that nothing was being reported on it in the news.

She'd never heard a hungover Davic before and decided she didn't need to scold him.

At the end of the day, the trade agreement was signed in a big ceremony held in the Yellow Room, then the Canadians headed for the airport for their flight back to Ottawa.

Rain moved into D.C. as the evening progressed.

Beau sat in the Oval Office, reviewing the CIA background check on Davic that Bowser had retrieved for him. Bowser sat on the sofa across from Beau's desk.

"An intelligence officer turned political aide for the Prime Minister?" Beau said rhetorically. "Deliciously interesting."

"We should sweep the House for bugs," Bowser said.

"Good for starts," Beau said. "Why is CSIS on top of him, is he under investigation?"

"The station chief wasn't forthcoming," Bowser said. "He's under something that sounds like a plea agreement. CSIS can pull him anytime they want, probation of sorts. "

"Clearly he lied on his background check.What were his intentions?" Beau said, shuffling the papers.

"His official file is sealed. I gather he was a tech but got booted out, no idea why."

"That's a huge red flag," Beau said.

"I don't know his game but something is rotten," Bowser said.

"If he goes on the record of what happened here, we can't paint him as just another tin-hat conspiracy theorist," Beau said. "You can color outside the lines on this one."

Bowser left the office as Beau poured himself a Chivas at the wet bar.

The possibilities were endless. Was all this part of some long game? Was Innis a Machiavellian genius?

Or maybe Davic worked for someone higher than Innis, unknown to her.

"Mrs. Van Alden?" he said into phone.

"Yes, Mr. President?"

"Contact Ambassador Whiteberry in Ottawa"

"Right away, Mr. President."

He couldn't imagine Jordan knowingly working to undermine him. She was something rare, a politician who didn't pull punches. She was a breath of fresh air. It reminded him why he got into politics. She was so young and energetic. She truly believed her policies would change the world for the better.

"Mr. President, Ambassador Whiteberry on the line."

Beau switched lines.

"Hello, Ambassador, I think we need to have a talk about Jordan Innis."

Chapter 4: Fostering Hope

Davic's grandfather died when he was 11, then his grandmother when he was 15. Davic was flown from his rural hometown to a foster-care facility in Ottawa. It was the first time he'd been on a flight and the woman who escorted him as far as the security gate put a tag around his neck with 'David Woods' on it. He tore it off as soon as she left but held onto it, his identification once he arrived in Ottawa to be picked up by two women from the facility.

He was given a physical immediately upon his arrival and he was 80 pounds underweight.

After his grandfather's death, Davic's grandmother's mental health had deteriorated at an incredible rate, to the point that for the past three years, Davic had had to fend for himself in terms of food. He satisfied his school requirements by correspondence school. He'd turned the barn into a slaughterhouse where he hung and dressed the carcasses of small animals he killed and cooked. Davic withheld all this from the facility administrators, but an investigation of the house revealed most of it anyhow.

Davic wouldn't remain in foster care for very long. Within a week of his arrival, he was informed that his adoption by a family - the Drews - had been approved, a remarkable turnaround, the social worker told Davic, a miracle.

Cy and Lemma Drew lived in suburban Ottawa, in a beautiful two-story home. They were very welcoming to Davic, who entered their house holding the framed photo of his family. They showed him his room and left him to unpack.

Davic had graduated the previous spring and was due to start online classes with the University of Ottawa in the fall. In the meantime he occupied himself by creating programs and algorithms to collect various information from websites and compile it for simple browsing.

He and Cy easily bonded over their shared passion for computers and programming, and Cy soon talked with his boss at CSIS about opportunities for Davic to get involved, perhaps an internship.

Cy had worked his way up to the upper end of middle management for the technology department in CSIS. He had few direct dealings with the director, so he was confused and concerned when he walked in one day to find a note on his desk asking him to go to the director's office straight away.

He walked in not knowing what to expect.

"Sit," ordered the director.

Drew did as asked.

"None of what we're about to discuss is to leave this room."

Who would Cy tell? Lemma and Davic seemed harmless recipients. Nonetheless, he nodded.

"You have been specifically requested by one of our suppliers," the director said. Drew shook his head confused.

"Who?"

"Viking."

Viking? That was their biggest supplier. What in the world could the owner want with Cy?

"The owner insists going by the name Thor. The Five Eyes have a deal to help protect him and in exchange he sells only to us."

The Five Eyes, or FVEY, was an alliance of the intelligence agencies of Australia, New Zealand, Canada, the UK, and the US. The information gathered and shared among these agencies was integral in maintaining national and international security and FVEY's monopoly on

Viking's state-of-the-art technology ensured continued supremacy.

"For whatever reason he has requested you to be his contact person with CSIS," the director said.

"What will that entail?"

"He'll be here today after lunch. I'll send someone for you when he arrives. He'll show you what he has and you pass along the info. Simple."

Cy agreed and after reaffirming the secrecy of this information, he was dismissed. He was greeted by the office secretary as he passed.

"How's David, Cy?"

"Dav*ic*. He's good."

Davic had lived with Cy and Lemma now for three months.

"Not driving you crazy yet?" the secretary asked. "Teens can be a handful."

"I'll look forward to that."

Sure enough, just after lunch, he was summoned to the assistant director's office, which had been cleared out for the occasion. Security officers Cy had never seen before showed him into the office.

A man stood in a light gray overcoat looking out the window, whose blinds he turned up once Cy entered and the door closed behind him.

"Are you Cy Elia Drew?" the man asked, not looking at him.

"I am."

"Your wife, Lemma, is religious but not devout. She attends just about every mainstream religious service," the man continued.

"How she makes friends," Cy said, then added, "*and* hedges her bets for an after life."

The joke always elicited a laugh from their friends. This man, however, was unamused.

"You can call me Thor," the man said. "It's a joke in my family that got outta hand."

He turned around and shook Cy's hand.

"By the way, congratulations on becoming a father," Thor said. "Seems like a smart kid."

Cy wasn't surprised this man had as much information on his life as he did. What else could you expect from the owner of the most sophisticated intelligence-technology vendor in the world?

"Thanks," Cy said.

Thor smiled and pulled out a small plastic vial that looked like it contained glitter.

"Surveillance dust," he explained. "GPS and audio. We're working on video. Transfer by touch, live-stream to Viking's VPN and instant storage. Figured you would want to test it out."

A few nights after this, Cy, Lemma, and Davic were having dinner and in a lull in conversation, Davic said:

"You work for CSIS, don't you?"

Cy glanced up as though a huge secret of his had just been made public. Lemma knew but he had told Davic that he worked for a think-tank simply because there was currently no reason for him to know otherwise.

"What makes you think that?" Drew asked.

Davic didn't act accusatory or behave as though he'd uncovered something to shame Cy with. He simply stated a question whose answer he already knew and wanted Cy to confirm himself.

"It took me a while to break the encryption but I got in," Davic said casually.

Drew shook his head.

"There's no way."

"I did," Davic said, shrugging.

Cy's face turned red. He got up from the table and headed upstairs, Davic following, not trying to stop him. In

Davic's room, Cy opened Davic's laptop and immediately saw emails from Cy's CSIS server were in a native inbox on Davic's computer.

"Oh shit…"

Cy's fingers thumped Davic's keyboard as he frantically cleaned out the emails.

"Why did you do this?" he demanded.

"I…was just testing out a program."

"Do you know what you've *done*? This is *illegal.*"

Once the emails had been deleted, Cy went to his office across the hallway. Davic remained in his room, awaiting his punishment.

It had only been a few months. Would they send him back to foster care?

The thought made Davic want to cry. He hadn't meant to do anything illegal, to hurt Cy's job. But once he'd encountered the Viking encryption, Davic had become obsessed with trying to break through it. And he had. And then he'd just wanted to know the truth about his foster father's job. Working for a national intelligence agency, to Davic, was the coolest job in the world.

Fifteen minutes later Cy returned to Davic's bedroom and ordered him to follow. Cy picked up Davic's laptop and headed downstairs and out to the car.

Cy pulled into the CSIS parking lot, in his stall, and took the laptop with him into the building, Davic hurrying up behind him. Cy flashed his credentials to the front-desk guard, then headed for the elevators and once alone in the car, Cy broke his silence.

"You're going to explain everything to the director, answer him honestly."

Davic's fear now had an endpoint and he wasn't sure if that was better than the dread and doubt he'd felt on the way to the CSIS office.

The offices were empty but the director's door was open and he sat behind his desk, waiting. Cy and Davic entered, Cy instructing Davic to sit while he handed Davic's laptop to the director.

At the director's insistence, Davic explained what he'd done and what he'd seen - only an email about "surveillance glitter."

After a 10-minute interrogation, the director took away the laptop and Cy and Davic went to his office, where they waited. At midnight they ordered Chinese delivery from down the road.

"Regardless of what happens, I think your job is cool," Davic said as they ate, waiting for the director to return.

"I love you, regardless, but this is very serious," Drew said.

"I know."

An hour later, the director returned with a programmer named Henry, and asked Davic to follow Henry while the director and Cy talked.

"We're trying to interpret the program but yes, he breached the server," the director said.

"What do you wanna do?" Cy asked.

"I'm not mad," the director said. "He's just a kid too smart for his own good. I wanna give him a job, put his skills to use. Viking isn't the most user-friendly software and our guys could use some help fixing the way he got in."

Cy was elated and knew Davic would be too.

Davic had been working at CSIS for two years in server maintenance.

"Hey, wizkid" said Shipley, who was in his late-20s, standing outside Davic's cubicle.

Davic was familiar with him only because he'd seen his file repeatedly but as far as Davic could recall, he and Shipley had never formally met.

"Your Drew's kid, right?"

Davic nodded.

"Down in operations we have a bet you could help clear up. How old are you?"

"17."

"Everyone else thought you were like 15. Anyway, you just won me a case of beer. You wanna swing by around five to hang out?"

Davic wondered if Shipley's case of beer would also be there. He'd never tried alcohol and didn't want to, especially at his adopted father's work. But this was a chance for him to make friends, so he agreed.

And indeed the beer was being passed around. Shipley gave Davic a can and he politely took a sip to satisfy Shipley, then hid the can as Shipley talked with his colleagues in operations.

"We're heading out on the town," Shipley said. "You wanna come?"

"Sure, lemme just let Mr. Drew know.'

"I already told him," Shipley said. "He said it's fine since you're with us."

They headed out into the parking lot and got into a surveillance van. Davic was apprehensive, wondering why they wouldn't go in one of their own vehicles, but Shipley pulled him into the vehicle.

Shipley drove while the two other men crouched in the back of the van in front of monitors, putting on headsets.

Shipley drove them into downtown Ottawa and parked on the curb, both sides filled with nightclubs. No one had said a word since getting into the van. Now Shipley handed Davic a pair of ripped jeans and a faded logo T-shirt.

"Put this on."

"I...prefer my suit."

"David—"

"Dav*ic*."

"*Davic*," Shipley corrected himself. "See, the thing is, I've been after this pedophile ring for a while. The guy I need is gonna be in that club down there tonight, see it?

The Silver."

Shipley pointed and Davic saw: a typical club façade, uncrowded currently, nothing about it to suggest the ulterior purpose Shipley was talking about.

"I don't know…" Davic said.

"Just wear a recorder in your backpack," Shipley said. "I'll be in there with you and you just act like a teenager, OK? You know how to act like a teenager? Just look at your phone a lot."

Davic looked up again at the club.

"We have to help those kids," Shipley said.

Davic nodded and took the clothes. In 45 minutes Davic was at Shipley's side as he knocked on the door of the club.

"Hey, I'm Sven, a friend of Lyle's," Shipley said to the bouncers who answered the door of the as-yet unopened club. "This is Josh, it's his first time."

The bouncers admitted the two into the hallway of the silent, empty club. While they patted "Sven" down, they groped through Davic's jeans and T-shirt. He wanted to strike back but knew he couldn't blow their cover.

The bouncers led the two into the front room of the club: the dancing platform was being swept and the bar restocked for the evening ahead.

A man emerged from a back room.

"Sven?" he asked Shipley.

"Yes, sir."

"Good to finally put a face to the name," Lyle said. "And Josh?"

Davic said nothing as Lyle's eyes landed on him.

"Of course," Shipley said. "He doesn't speak much English."

Lyle chuckled.

"Well, that's OK. He's a little older than I prefer but cute. Tell him to go to the back with the others."

Shipley turned Davic to face him and spoke in a fast, staccato language Davic didn't understand but could tell

54

from Shipley's arm motions that he was supposed to go back the way Lyle had come and Davic did, moving unsurely both for effect and because he was.

Shipley and Lyle sat at a table to talk money.

In the back room were eight kids - new deliveries - ages ranging from six to 15. Some were dark-skinned and only a few spoke English. They played with each other, unconcerned, perhaps thinking they were in some kind of daycare, not yet privy to the knowledge of where they were headed.

Davic turned around several times, allowing the camera and recorder in his backpack to get a full view, just as he'd been instructed to do.

These kids would likely end up in foster care after this. He hoped they would find their own Mr. Drews. He wondered where he would be if the ministry had not sent him to the Drews. That thought opened the way for him to think about his father, which made his eyes tear up.

He couldn't think about that stuff now. Right then the kids needed his help and his full attention.

After 20 minutes of surveying the backroom, he heard Shipley call out to 'Josh.'

Davic turned around and found Lyle and Shipley just in the doorway. Shipley waved him over and said something else in his unfamiliar language, which translated to, "They don't have room in the van to transport you today, so we'll come back tomorrow, OK?"

Shipley nodded at the end of his sentence and Davic mimed him. Then Shipley and Lyle shook hands and Lyle took Davic's face between his hands, examining his features, then kissing his forehead.

"Until tomorrow."

Shipley and Davic headed back out of the club, Davic's skin trying to pull itself off his bones, and once back in the surveillance truck, Davic wiggled out of the backpack and tossed off the shirt with disgust. He changed back into his suit, then joined the others around the monitors. Seeing his trembling, Shipley put a can of beer in Davic's hand.

"You did good work. The Mounties're on their way and this place'll be shut down before the night's over."

It wasn't what Davic had expected. In the action movies he and the Drews sometimes watched, the hero, no matter his job, was always involved in the action, so Davic had thought he and Shipley would be the ones arresting the club owner.

But the more he thought about, the better off he thought he was: He didn't want to fight if he didn't have to. He was happy to be the eyes and ears and let the Mounties be the fists and teeth.

Chapter 5: Fatal Attraction

10 Downing Street was full of fanfare and cameras, the expected response to the occasion. The British Prime Minister had been in office long enough that this ritual was automatic. The tradition was for the two to shake hands in front of the door of Number 10 and Jordan did not disappoint, shaking hands with Basil Thatcher and smiling warmly into the cameras.

Basil was divorced so his daughter, Nigella, played the role of hostess and companion to her father to various social events. She was in the foyer of Number 10 to greet Jordan once she and Basil entered, then headed for the Prime Minister's office.

Davic came in behind Jordan and could not help admiring the beautiful Nigella. She caught his gaze and smiled back. Davic blushed, then forced his gaze back down to his omnipresent BlackBerry.

Davic made a point of adding to the conversation in Basil's office, though he felt Nigella's eyes on him the whole time and he struggled not to sweat. The events at the White House made him paranoid that even glancing at the Prime Minister's daughter would set off a sequence of events that would damage relations between Canada and the UK. Nigella's tabloid-given reputation as a man-eater made him even more nervous. And he would not put it past Basil to have Davic drawn and quartered if anything happened, public scandal or not.

Jordan noted Davic's uncharacteristically rigid posture and monotone voice. It was a friendly gathering with light conversation but something had him spooked.

Halfway through the conversation, Basil grinned. He had figured out why Jordan's aide was blushing and he also knew what Nigella was thinking. The upside of her being interested in a political aide, as opposed to the semi-celebrities she typically went after, was that it was not likely to wind up in the tabloids, if Jordan's description of Davic were to be trusted.

Davic did not fit what Basil had thought was his daughter's type: He was tall, blond, with a youthful face, rimless glasses magnifying his pale blue eyes, with a smooth-faced watch that was not an Apple Watch - Basil presumed it was a device of Davic's own making. All in all he lacked the element of danger and excitement that had been a common thread throughout Nigella's flings and so he was the first Basil immediately approved of.

The relationship between Jordan and Davic was one Basil had not encountered before: Both contributed nearly the same amount to the conversation with Basil. Clearly, despite his nerdy exterior, Davic carried and conducted himself as an alpha male, not the typical subservient political aide.

And both were young, so Jordan's ascension to the Prime Minister's office was still more baffling. Research by MI6 into her campaign had revealed no major donors - it had mostly been a grassroots campaign that had gone viral. Basil was sure Davic had been instrumental in that: From what he remembered from his briefing notes on Jordan and her staff, Davic had worked for some time with CSIS, which had lent him to the UK shortly before he'd left working in intelligence. Whatever Davic had done while in the UK hadn't been included in the report, but Basil could find out if he wanted to, though he was sure it was probably some kind of analytical work.

Still, Davic was the unknown variable in this mystery equation. Jordan acted and spoke on her own, so if Davic were playing her, she was at least unwitting as to her function in the game.

But Basil considered his own jaded nature in his thoughts about Davic: He was an enigma but maybe for once he wasn't of the nefarious type the international political world was rife with.

At last the informal meeting was over and Davic seemed relieved. Basil gave him a half-grin, which brought about an unsure expression on Davic's face. Basil enjoyed this brief manipulation of another man's emotions.

After the Canadians left, Basil requested Smyth, his liaison with the Secret Intelligence Service (SIS), to bring the original files and his notes on Davic. It contained little more information than Basil already had - Davic had graduated from high school at 15 and from the University of Ottawa at 17 with dual bachelor's in math and economics, then a master's at 19 in computer science. Basil learned Davic's family history and his job title at CSIS had been 'technical analyst.' Just two years after he'd left CSIS for unspecified reasons, Jordan had been elected as Prime Minister.

The only person more powerful than the king was the kingmaker. Was Davic the kingmaker of Canada?

Jordan was the front and Davic was likely the brains. Some people want power but not the spotlight that frequently accompanies it. Davic fit that.

How did Jordan's American "husband" fit in?

He was part of the media but surely Jordan must know everything about him, perhaps Davic too.

Some sort of alliance between America and Canada, deeper maybe than NATO, NAFTA, the UN, FVEY, was not necessarily a malevolent prospect but anyone would and should be suspicious.

He called Nigella into his office.

"The Canadian aide, Davic," Basil started. "Be careful with him. He's not just a staffer."

"He's her boy toy?" Nigella asked, slightly disappointed.

"No, I don't think so. We just have to regard him as

equal to Madam Innis."

His daughter was frowning.

"I did not say 'no,'" Basil said. "Just remember he's not some minor bureaucrat."

"Well...could you at least let him know you're not going to kill him?"

The bait was hooked. Basil was not concerned about Nigella's safety, not only because Davic did not seem the type capable of inflicting physical violence on someone else - Nigella likely had the weight advantage - but also because he would have Smyth keep an eye on them together. With Nigella as his bait, Basil could gain insights into Davic's daily activities. As a former intelligence officer himself, Davic might sense he was being spied on if Basil gave SIS direct orders to do so. The best spy was the unwitting spy and if she could appeal to his male tendencies, all the better for cover.

That night the Canadians prepared to attend a reception at Number 10 in their honor.

They were running late because Rigo had gone out around London. Jordan and Davic were already dressed when he returned and Davic and Alexandra Potvin, Jordan's administration's protocol officer, responsible for quickly educating any of the administration who went abroad on customs and social niceties, rushed him upstairs to get him dressed.

Potvin and Davic were equally irritated.

"The Brits are all about being fashionably late," Jordan said as the other two hauled Rigo upstairs. "Don't worry."

On the journey up the stairs, Potvin berated Rigo in English and French – she was from Montreal - about his insensitivity, so typically American, and reasoned aloud how he should wear his tuxedo.

Davic, while irritated that Rigo was late, was also pleased that Potvin was so bothered. He didn't much care for the protocol officer because of her strictness to abiding by social norms and rituals and when these were violated, which, for Davic, was - he was not the typical aide, after all, he was Jordan's right hand - her temper would flare. She and Davic had a number of arguments, some of which culminated in Potvin cursing him out in French, but Potvin had been retained in her position. Regardless of her temper, she was good at her job and dedicated.

The reception was largely leisure and an opportunity for Jordan to hobnob while for Davic it was work. He talked with various staff from the Commonwealth of Nations and ministries to set up meetings.

During his criss-crossing of the ballroom, he looked around but could not spot Nigella, whom he hoped was too busy hosting. It was irrational - he could not even look at her without a rush of fear coming over him.

It wasn't until he stopped at the bar for a glass of water that he saw peacock feathers above the crowd bobbing in his direction and below them was the mousy-haired Nigella.

How could he have missed her with those feathers? In any case it was too late. The most he could hope for now was to come up with a way to politely excuse himself and run out of Number 10.

"I was wondering if you were here," Nigella said, raising an eyebrow. "What's your mission this evening?"

She closed in, putting a hand on his on the bar.

Davic wondered at this statement. His 'mission?' Did she think he was some kind of spy, like James Bond? If he could be likened to any Ian Fleming character, Davic thought it would be Agent Q, the only thing interesting about whom was the technology he designed.

Of course his designing didn't have the resources of MI6 that Q had. If Nigella liked him simply because she thought he was a dangerous international man of mystery, she'd be disappointed once she realized he was just a boring tech nerd working in politics, less interesting and relatable than those she'd encountered as the Prime Minister's daughter before.

Nonetheless, the fact she was practically dangling herself in front of him - a deer begging the hunter for his gun so she could kill herself for him - affected him. He was slow in responding to her, trying to let his logical mind catch up.

"Miss Thatcher. I love your hat," he said, pointing to the feathers. "I would love to stay and chat but..." he grabbed his phone and faked reading a message. "Oh, look at that, I'm afraid duty calls."

He slipped his hand out from under hers and sidestepped her.

"Perhaps we'll run into each other later and chat," he added without thinking, immediately regretting it.

He disappeared into the crowd.

"My daughter has taken quite a liking to Davic," Basil said to Jordan and Rigo, chatting against a wall. "Perhaps you noticed."

"I did."

"Is he dating anyone?" Basil asked, unused to posing questions outright instead of employing mind games, a change he enjoyed.

"Only his BlackBerry," Rigo inserted.

They shared a chuckle.

"Unless Adam Smith is one of Nigella's favorite love poets, Davic can be a bit boring," Rigo continued.

"I'm afraid I haven't kept up with my daughter's literary tastes," Basil said.

Jordan smiled, taking out her phone and texting Davic, who, despite vanishing, just as easily rematerialized beside their group.

The events at the White House had served as a wake-up

call, at least for Jordan, that Davic needed a life outside of work. Knowing someone found him attractive, and that her very powerful father was supportive of the attraction, may inspire Davic.

"Basil and I were having a discussion about Adam Smith," she said to Davic, "How his work contributed to the end of slavery."

Rigo, though understanding this was just a pretext, was confused.

"Abraham Lincoln ended slavery," he said.

The group laughed, then Davic started explaining Smith's economic theory on slavery and why freemen labor was cheaper and better. "The UK stated clamping down on the slave trade in 1807 and then spent 5% of its GDP in 1833 to free any remaining slaves. They only repaid the loan in 2015."

Basil texted Nigella and before Davic could get into the history of property rights of the time, Rigo's eyes were glazing over.

Davic stopped mid-sentence when Nigella joined them.

"Ah, the invisible hand," she said. "The unintended benefits in a laissez-faire society"

Davic glanced at Basil uneasily, assuming the stiff pose that he'd had earlier during the meet-and-greet.

Basil was surprised Nigella had any clue who Adam Smith was. He suspected it had more to do with Adam Smith being on the 20-pound note than studies of *The Wealth of Nations*. In any case he put a hand on Davic's shoulder, introduced the two as a formality, then instructed Davic to go with Nigella to get a refill of what he thought was Davic's gin and tonic.

That veiled instruction, the hand on his shoulder, and a knowing wink was all Davic needed.

That evening Davic stayed at Number 10, and the next morning, Davic woke Jordan up with a phone call to give her the itinerary for the day.

Chapter 6: Boffin in Britain

Davic received a promotion and had been upgraded from a cubicle to his own office in the CSIS server room. The office wasn't much bigger than the cubicle but having a door made him feel like someone important.

The FVEY had an exchange program, in which staffers of each intelligence agency involved could apply to transfer and work for a different agency in any of the five countries. This was how older people or those whose skills didn't have any relevance in the fast-changing world of security technology anymore were phased out. 'Dance of the lemons,' Davic's supervisor had called it.

But Davic applied to the program, hoping to transfer to someplace his connection to Cy Drew would not be known. He was 22 and wanted to be treated as his own man. The expensive suit he wore helped but it was still not enough to overcome his baby face and his foster father's shadow.

As they drove home one day, Cy said he'd heard about Davic applying for the program. He didn't sound concerned or discouraging to Davic, only kind of sad.

"The tech department will be at a loss without you," Cy said. "And I'd miss you."

"The contracts are only a few months," Davic said. "It won't be long."

They were already talking as though Davic had been accepted. And of course that was because it wasn't a matter of 'if.' Davic was a master of Viking and had a standing offer from the owner, Thor, to come work for him, of which he reminded Davic whenever he came to vend new wares. Davic so far had declined, though working for Viking would entail more money, more responsibility. When Cy asked him why he was still at CSIS, Davic told him the story of going with Shipley to the club and getting the information needed for RCMP to shut down the child trafficker. Working toward a purpose that wasn't about profit appealed to Davic more.

A month later he had an interview at the British High Commision. The Government Communications Headquarters in Cheltenham was interested in bringing him over and the interview was part of his background check. His interview was with a woman named Poppy Baker-Finch, a beautiful woman in a black sheath dress embroidered with vibrant red poppies along the hemline and a matching red blazer. She was suspicious of his credentials and qualifications, considering he was only 22.

When she realized he was legitimate, a "kid genius," though Davic was quick to assure her that his rural upbringing provided little more stimulation than what he could find in chores, homework, and books, she took him to get polygraphed. Before he left she told him he would get a letter in a few weeks informing him of their decision.

None of the other agencies contacted him, probably for the same reason Poppy had at first been suspicious. Davic hadn't thought before that his qualifications wouldn't be taken seriously, as though his application were some joke by CSIS.

He and Cy were having lunch in Davic's office when the secretary dropped off a letter from the BHC. They stared at it on the edge of the desk.

"Don't keep me in suspense," Cy said.

Davic rolled his eyes.

"You open it."

Cy did.

"You better start drinking tea," Cy said, his eyes rising from the letter's first paragraph, smiling.

A month later Davic was at orientation for GCHQ. A man named Burk, from Australia, introduced himself as they sat next to each other. He was in his 40s, burly, and worked mostly in database administration for the Australian Signals Directorate.

At lunch he told Davic how his ex-wife had been promoted to the head of his department, thus he had applied for exchange.

"I know the Brits run little tests to see how people react," Burk said. "I'm trying to figure what they're testing with you."

Davic had no idea how to respond to this.

After lunch the exchanges learned GCHQ's reporting structure, then moved onto personal protection, how to identify Romeos or Catherine Tramells - spies who seduced staffers to get info on their departments.

Oscar, the orientation leader, was up front going over the PowerPoint when someone came in and handed him a thumb drive and whispered into his ear. He took the drive back to his desk.

"Woods to MI5."

The others exchanged looks but kept silent. Davic still felt embarrassed, like getting called to the principal's during primary school. He gathered his things and followed the man who had come in.

Down a row of cubicles, Davic smelled burning plastic and hair. The officer turned into one cubicle and Davic saw, on the desk, was a fire-blackened desktop computer and beside it, the scorched remnants of his own laptop.

"This the guy?" asked an angry-looking man behind the desk. "He's a *kid*."

Still, he motioned Davic to sit and the man that had led him left.

"You hospitalized one of my men," the angry man said.

"Maybe next time you break into my apartment and take my computer to secretly run scans on it, you should tell me," Davic said, uncomfortably chuckling.

The man was not amused.

"Is your guy going to be OK?"

"He has burns on his hands."

"It discharges the battery capacity, frying any connected devices. Pretty good security technology, if you ask me: Protect the data and mark the guy trying to break in."

The man was not relinquishing any of his anger.

"Well, it's just a prototype. Hold on."

Davic plugged in his laptop: Part of the screen was dead but it booted up and allowed Davic access.

"There are a couple projects using Viking," Davic said, turning the laptop toward the now pensive man. "Didn't think just a password or two was safe enough."

"Mind if I get a boffin to look at it?" he asked.

Davic agreed.

When the man, whose anger had leveled off, returned, he brought another tech who knew Viking, though not as much as Davic, who enjoyed explaining his project almost as much as the intrigued tech liked listening.

Oscar appeared a little later and explained that, while CSIS used Viking to encode their data, Britain used it only for their most classified information. Because of this, Oscar thought Davic would be more of an asset in one of the departments that directly handled Viking-level information, which would require a higher level of clearance.

After Davic agreed, they went to the Fiddlehead Pub, where Burk was buying the techs rounds to keep them from talking about the cuck porn they found on his home computer.

Col. Randall Smyth woke in a sweat. He assured himself he was in a single officers barracks back in the UK. He knew while he was here, people in Afghanistan were being tortured to death - people he knew and had promised he would help in exchange for information.

Smyth made his way to his temporary office. The

bureaucracy was obstructing his ability to root out the Butchers. It should have been done a long time ago, they should never have been able to build their ranks to the point they were at now. He dialed the phone.

"Oscar, Smyth, Intel Corps. Did you get the specifications I sent?"

"Yes, I did. I'm not sure we have the tech you need."

Smyth sighed heavily. He'd heard this so often but each time he'd been able to find a way around it. This was the last piece, what would enable them to at last stamp out the Butchers.

"I'm desperate, Oscar," Smyth said, his voice going down an octave. "You know what we're trying to do."

"Yeah," Oscar said, his tone following Smyth's. "The Canadians are further ahead. They may have the tech you need in theater. And we just cleared a Canadian to work the equipment."

"Where is he?"

"Here. But he's—"

"I'll be there shortly," Smyth said and hung up.

Smyth sat in Oscar's office after he went to retrieve Davic.

Smyth saw the families strung up by barbed wire around their limbs from his dreams. Forensic reports had shown they had been alive when the mutilation occurred. Each incident was getting more brazen and sadistic, which understandably made the locals more reluctant to talk to his people.

Oscar and Davic arrived and Oscar introduced Davic to Smyth, who at first thought the Boy was someone's son visiting.

"What are you looking for?" Davic asked.

Smyth gave him a sheet of paper.

"You understand we're going to be out in theater?" Smyth asked, wondering if the Boy even knew what 'theater' meant.

"Of course," Davic said, looking over the paper.

"Will there be any issues getting the equipment from CSIS stations?"

"They'll scan my ID and biometrics," Davic said.

"And you can operate all that?"

"I was part of the programming team."

"When can you start?"

Davic looked at Oscar, who was reluctant to say anything.

"Can fly out later today if you can get packed," Smyth said

"Davic," Oscar said, "Smyth and I need to talk."

Davic nodded and left the office.

"I don't think he's suited," Oscar said

"He's everything I need."

"His father is someone. If this goes sideways, there'll be hell to pay."

"He will be surrounded by Marines."

"They'll eat him alive."

"I have good people dying for trying to help me. You want those fancy servers? I get my Butchers, I'll raise your budget."

Oscar pondered

"It's up to him," Oscar said.

The next day, they were in Afghanistan, and Davic followed Smyth across the tarmac after disembarking from the C-130J. Davic smiled, watching the men salute Smyth as they proceeded through camp.

Immediately the first order was to take Davic to the nearby CSIS station to check out the equipment Smyth needed. After this they proceeded to the forward operating base.

Smyth ordered two Marines, Cook and Kenworth, to transport Davic, who was intimidated by the two large men.

"We have a car seat for the humvee?" Kenworth asked Cook, smirking at Davic.

Once they were in the truck and driving toward the Canadian camp, Cook turned to Davic in the back seat.

"So what brings you here? The mission was green lighted suddenly, we using you as bait?"

"I hope not. I'm a tech. I'm looking after some equipment," Davic said.

At the station Davic was in and out quickly, the Marines helping him carry the equipment.

The FOB was a walled villa surrounded by an area that may have been a garden at one point but the dead, sand-overrun area was currently used for storage of supplies. Davic was given a room in the villa for his office and he went about setting up the equipment.

The team medic introduced himself as Rossco, second-in-command, saying dinner would be mutton.

"You're the first spy I've met besides the commander," Rossco said.

"I'm just a tech. Nice to meet you," Davic said, shaking his hand.

Rossco told Davic to report for a physical after dinner, then he would spar with the soldiers in the morning. Rossco then led Davic to his bunk, in one of a couple rooms that had been furnished with stark bunks and lockers crammed against the walls.

Beside the room was the "water closet," as Rossco called it, wherein a man stood in front of the mirror shaving.

Across the hall was Smyth's quarters and beside that the infirmary, Rossco's office.

Rossco said he hoped Smyth's mission would be over in the next three months. Then Rossco could write to the medical board and become a full-fledged doctor. He had a building in mind for his practice and had a recurring dream of hanging his medical degree upon the wall.

In the mess hall, soldiers dished out food to other soldiers, who sat on pillows on the floor.

"Hey Brown," Cook said to one of the cooks. "Gotta high chair for the Boy?"

The other soldiers, gathered around Cook on the floor, snickered. Cook handed Davic a plate of food, winked so that Davic knew he was just busting his chops.

"I wanna make the guys breakfast tomorrow," Davic said to Rossco. "Would that be OK?"

"Sure," Rossco said. "Spare them eating what I make."

Smyth walked in briefly to get a plate of food, and the heads in the mess hall turned, voices dying down. Davic saw Smyth's brow was crinkled and he said nothing to anyone before he headed back to his office.

"What's this mission all about?" Davic asked, realizing he hadn't been told anything besides his own function as part of this team.

The men around him stirred the food around on their plates or clinked their silverware on the edges, a tangible pall coming over them.

Cook then started elaborating.

Chapter 7: Dropping the Hammer and Sickle

That year's G20 summit took place in Toronto at the Metro Convention Centre and was yet another event that brought out the protesters, some representing only themselves, others representing loose collections that interacted only on the internet, and still others, larger and older groups, such as the Front de libération du Québec. The FLQ was established back in the '60s and over the decades had perpetrated violent crimes for the sake of rebelling against "Anglo-Saxon imperialism" and establishing a Québec sovereignty free of Canadians.

Contrasting the violence invoked by these black-clothed groups, some wearing red bandanas, others balaclavas, which included setting cars on fire, assaulting passersby on the street, fist-fighting with members of other groups whose ideologies differed only a little, were the peaceful protesters. These, many in tye-dye or bright-colored clothing, marched around the convention center, led by organizers with megaphones chanting various phrases, which the followers repeated.

All taunted the RCMP stationed at various points in and around the convention center, but only the most belligerent and violent were confronted, chased, beaten, handcuffed, and jailed.

Rigo worried about being the only male spouse of a world leader. Thankfully no one noticed when he wandered out of events in the convention center. Even Davic and Potvin were not on his case for some breach of protocol, a rare thing.

Wandering around the halls of the convention center,

trying to find someplace to get coffee but all the vendors were closed, he spotted a young man sitting on a bench with *L'Équipe,* a French daily sports newspaper.

"Parlez anglais?" Rigo asked, virtually the extent of his French.

The young man glanced over the edge of the paper, nodded.

"How 'bout them Yanks?" Rigo asked, hoping the young man were a soccer fan and had seen the recent game between the American Yanks and France's Blues.

"Lloris couldn't catch a metal ball with magnetic hands."

Rigo laughed and he and the young man, who turned out to be a French diplomat's son, continued talking for a while. In addition to sports, they both had a thirst for coffee in common and the younger man gave Rigo the address for a coffee shop a healthy distance away from the convention center. They planned to ditch their respective handlers and meet in an hour.

Alexandra Potvin intercepted him in the hallway of the hotel after he'd gone to change into more casual clothes.

"Where have you been?" she asked in that shrill voice Rigo had come to hate.

"Staying out of the limelight."

"Where are you going?"

"To get coffee, that all right with you, Mother?" Rigo said, not caring his tone was sarcastic and hostile. Potvin had always treated him like a tempestuous child and not the spouse of a world leader.

"Where?"

"Someplace, here's the address."

He handed her the piece of paper the diplomat's son had written on. Then she handed it back and let him go without another pestering word, a smug smile on her face as he left.

Back at the convention center, Davic had just realized Rigo was nowhere to be found. Jordan had no idea where he went and all the other staffers could tell him was that they'd seen Rigo leave the event hall a couple hours ago.

As Davic stalked the halls of the convention center, he called Rigo but his phone immediately went to voicemail - it was either dead or off. He texted Rigo to check in with someone immediately, then called Potvin, who didn't answer. Captain Remy, head of Jordan's security detail, also had no idea of Rigo's whereabouts.

Finally after half an hour, Potvin called him back to tell him Rigo had gone to the coffee shop.

"Why would you let him go?" Davic hissed, finally able to chew out Potvin for a slip up as she had done to him numerous times before.

"I thought it was better than letting him hang around all the world's leaders!"

Davic looked up directions to the coffee shop on his BlackBerry, then rushed through a back entrance of the convention center, which, despite not being the primary entrance, was still patrolled by protesters kept in line by a few RCMP officers.

Working his way through the people, whose mass increased the farther he got from the convention center, he suddenly remembered the Armani suit he was wearing, making him stick out like a sore thumb and instantly identifying him as a member of the group many of these protesters despised. He was symbolically "the man" they wished to stick it to.

And the deeper he went into their ranks, the more attention he drew, which included various attempts to trip him, shoving and bumping him, cursing and hurling insults at him. Davic kept his head down, not engaging: Most of these people were just being victims for attention, knowing the press would feed that need and produce the desire for more.

"You racist pig!" someone screamed.

Davic just narrowly avoided a brick flying at him. A group of men broke apart to also evade the brick as it came their way, then reassembled, shouting, demanding to know who had thrown the projectile. A man emerged from another group timidly, trying to explain that he had thrown the brick at Davic, who, sensing escalation, slipped away, so when the other group tried to locate him, they instead accused the other group of lying and being cowards. And indeed this led to escalation, with both groups screaming 'racist' and 'fascist' at each other, until they engaged with fists and kicks.

The brawling caused others in the mass of people to take sides, so within two minutes, more than 400 people were fighting blindly, for no reason other than that they could.

In the havoc, as Davic kept himself as low as possible, he was caught by what felt like a cannonball to his side and collapsed. His lungs were paralyzed, rendering him incapable of breathing, and then he felt a foot on his back, pinning him to the pavement. The pressure intensified, and he could not draw a breath. Then Davic felt cool steel on the back of his head. The pressure on his back eased up as his assailant reared up - Davic could imagine he was raising a hammer, preparing to bring it down to smash into Davic's skull - but his attacker was bombarded by another group bashing him with their protest signs. These weren't very potent attacks but distracted the attacker enough to allow Davic to scramble to his feet and run away.

He kept his direction only by looking at the map on his phone, otherwise the unfaltering density of people would have rendered him lost. A woman in a Che Guevara T-shirt and aquamarine hair was shoved onto her back by two men and before he could think twice about it, Davic offered her his hand. The woman took it, then just as quickly punched him in the face before running off. The punch wasn't very strong, just lucky - for her - as Davic immediately felt blood pouring down his face and onto his suit.

His ears were ringing - numbed by the screaming all around.

Rigo was ahead of Davic by about a half-mile, taking side alleys to avoid the protesters along the main route leading to the coffee shop. So far he'd gotten in no altercations, though he could hear the protesters turning into rioters behind him and this made him move faster.

"Rigo Innis?" a voice called to him from down a side path he passed without looking down.

When he glanced that way, he saw three men in black, their faces covered with balaclavas, and instantly Rigo was scared.

How did they know who he was - even though they'd gotten his last name wrong? He'd purposely changed his clothes and put on a hat in order not to stand out, he just wanted to be normal.

The three men kept on the approach, moving cautiously as hunters toward a deer.

Rigo broke into a run, heading for an alley ahead by which he could access a main road.

"That's him," he heard one of the men say, followed by their boots clomping as they dashed after him.

One man followed Rigo down the alley he headed for while the other two circled around by going down a second lower alley. Hearing the footsteps decrease in number behind him, Rigo understood the implication and as he neared the end of his alley, he lowered his head and bunched up his shoulders, preparing to barrel through the other two men, who were surely going to ambush him.

He was right: As soon as he emerged, the other two masked men pounced on him from either side and he would have been able to escape them if the third man hadn't been so close behind. With the two trappers killing his momentum, Rigo was a sitting duck and easily taken down by the third man tackling him.

The street was empty, the shops closed down early because of fear of the protesters, so Rigo's cries for help went unanswered. The three men picked him up by his legs and arms, rushing him through the crossroads, and just as they got upon the opposite sidewalk, they heard the sirens of an RCMP unit - which had previously been heading for the convention center but had detoured at the sight of three men in black struggling to keep Rigo's thrashing under control.

The sirens were closing in and one of the men swore. "Ditch him!"

The men dropped Rigo face-first onto the sidewalk, then bolted. One of the men took out a walkie-talkie.

"Abort, take off!" Rigo heard the man yell into the device.

They vanished up an alley, no doubt headed for the madness of the protesters, where they could disappear.

The RCMP unit screeched to a stop beside Rigo and two officers got out, asking if he was OK and what had happened.

After verifying Rigo was the Prime Minister's husband, they drove him back to the hotel. On the drive over, Rigo turned on his phone and found a flurry of messages and voicemails from Davic and Remy.

He tried calling Davic but it went to voicemail after a half-dozen rings, so he called Remy who was furious at the situation. Remy insisted Davic, Jordan, and him needed to meet Rigo at the hotel. "I can't get a hold of Davic," Rigo said.

"Probably tried to go after you himself. Can't take him anywhere without trouble."

Remy hung up, then radioed his units around the convention center a description of Davic, giving the address of the coffee shop, which Rigo had given him.

One portion of the protesters had gotten so out of hand, RCMP officers had surrounded them, decked in riot gear and batons. They launched canisters of tear gas into the mob, which slowly broke up the violence, the protesters scattering, many evading arrest.

Davic - bloodied suit torn, face bruised - had snatched a bandana off the ground to guard his nose, mouth, and eyes against the fumes. An officer ran up behind him, ordering him to his knees, his hands above his head, and a glance over his shoulder gave Davic relief that it was, in fact, a law-enforcement officer and he complied. He was handcuffed and taken to a cruiser, where his ID was checked.

The officer, his helmet's visor raised, spoke into the radio on his shoulder:

"Tell Remy his MIA staffer's been found."

Remy's PPS officers escorted Davic up to Jordan's room, where she, Rigo, Remy, Alexandra Potvin, and the officers who had saved Rigo were already gathered.

The PPS officers had given Davic a water bottle to rinse off the blood from his face, as well as wash out the tear gas from his eyes and nose, but he still looked like he'd been sucked in and thrown up by a tornado. He walked into the room bracing his ribs from when he'd been struck.

"Trade deals can be brutal, huh?" he said, trying to break the palpable tension he felt.

Davic couldn't remember ever having seen so much worry on so many faces at one time.

"What happened?" Davic asked.

"Three men tried to kidnap Rigo," Jordan said, her voice shaky.

Davic was speechless. Rigo retold the events and Davic stopped him when he was talking about the French diplomat's son.

"Which diplomat?"

Rigo thought.

"Laurent."

"Laurent doesn't have a son," Davic said, remembering Laurent only had a 15-year-old daughter from the briefing notes.

This was news to the others and Rigo gave a description of the young man to the PPS and RCMP officers.

As Rigo continued his story, Davic remembered being struck, then pinned to the ground, the cool steel at the back of his head during the riot. He told those gathered about this once Rigo was done.

"This was coordinated," Jordan concluded.

After some speculation, Davic theorized the kidnap attempt originated in either the French or the Québec delegation, as Rigo swore the young man he'd encountered had an accent. France's president and Jordan had had no issues thus far. Nor had any of her trade policies rubbed any of France's political parties the wrong way.

Québec's premier, Françcois LaSalle, on the other hand, was adamantly and famously anti-American and had had no shortage of disparaging remarks about Jordan after it was revealed she was married to an American.

"Of course it could be a frame-up," Davic said. "LaSalle's the first person we'd suspect."

The RCMP called for a forensic artist to come to the hotel to draw up a rendering of Rigo's description of the man he'd met. With this, a person-of-interest notice would be put out to the public and Davic would send the rendering to the CSIS office in Montréal to run a facial-recognition scan.

In the privacy of his room, Davic checked the internet to see if word of Rigo's attempted abduction had gotten to the press. So far it hadn't. One less thing he had to play damage control on.

He needed rest. He'd refused Remy's advice he get checked out at the hospital. If his ribs didn't feel better in a week or so, he would consider it. For now, though, it was better to keep all this as contained as possible.

He took a shower to clean off the protester-grime and through the mist, he looked at the scar tissue encircling both his wrists, which he usually concealed with his watch band and long sleeves.

No matter how hard he'd thought about it in the past, he could never remember how he'd received them. He knew he hadn't always had them, nor even for a long period. These scars were really the only physical manifestation he had of the missing part of his memory.

From the looks of the pearly-colored tissue, it had been a violent event that had resulted in them.

As violent as today? Would he ever know?

The abduction attempt threatened ever finding out. Someone, or some people, someplace were conspiring against Jordan. Without Jordan in office, Davic's chances at getting access to his file were virtually nil.

Once out of the shower, he dressed in loose clothes - long sleeves - and once out of sight, the scars were out of his mind and he was able to sleep with the help of a few painkillers.

Chapter 8: Pyrrhic Victory

"We can't let him know what happened to him."

Smyth, in a hospital gown, stood at the side of a bed in a UK military aid post and held the hand of Davic, who was in a coma. He wasn't going to let the thought of the Boy not waking up cross his mind. He had pulled rank to get him the best care the post could offer.

Oscar's worst fear had come true but the possibility that the mission wouldn't be successful had never occurred to Smyth. But then the mission *had* been successful, though at great cost.

Davic never should have been in any combat situation. But then that wasn't necessarily true because, when it had come to combat, Davic had handled himself better than any of the soldiers could've predicted, given how easily they had been able to overpower him during their sparring practice.

The situation Davic had been in, which had led to his coma, none of the soldiers should ever have been in. But they all had and Davic had gotten the worst of it...because of Smyth. And the only reason any of them were still alive was Davic.

Any outsider who was not there would have a hard time believing the skinny boy single handedly saved the lives of the British Marines. Smyth's superiors were suspicious of his debrief, blaming the mental stress of the situation. It was only when it was corroborated by all his men that the truth accepted.

Cy was also in the room, his eyes red and swollen from crying. He wasn't crying now, just staring at the sight of his foster son - his *son* - in the bed, the heart monitor beeping rhythmically.

Blood-stained barbed wire lay coiled in a stainless steel

pan beside the bed. They had been unwound from Davic's wrists and ankles, a trademark of the Butchers. Davic and the Marines would forever carry the scars of this encounter physically.

Cy could only think about the 15-year-old Davic, smiling as they took a tour of the Canadian Parliament - Davic looking out from the observation deck of Peace Tower. Not in a million years would Cy have believed then that they would be here now: Davic dependent on a respirator.

All Smyth could think about was how he'd contributed to Davic's condition now. His anger had gotten the team captured. He should have ordered a retreat, would have in any other situation. But they had been so close to the Butchers - finally, after years - and Smyth's arrogance had led them straight into a trap.

"I know he'll wake up," Smyth said, incredulous that he actually believed this.

How would the Boy function *when* he woke up? He might be a vegetable, a husk. Would that be preferable to death? The Boy loved intelligence work and his body was not made for physical work to start with. What would his life be like?

Cy couldn't bear to voice any of the doubt he felt and hated himself for.

"*When* he wakes up," Smyth said, "we tell him nothing. If he remembers any of this, we'll deal with it, but if he doesn't, we don't tell him. You get this sealed and I'll get it classified. Deal?"

Smyth's confidence, contrived as it obviously was, spurred Cy to find some shred of hope, futile though it may be. He and Smyth shook hands.

Chapter 9: Delacroix to Bare

Two agents had been posted outside Jordan's room the whole night, and the morning after Rigo's attempted abduction, Davic went to Jordan's room with a black eye that had formed overnight. They had two hours before they had to go back to the convention center to attend a meeting with the Chinese delegation.

Despite yesterday's events, Rigo was in good spirits and was made more so watching Jordan apply cover-up to Davic's eye.

Toronto jails were overflowing with protester-prisoners today and security at the convention center had been upped, though it was now noon and almost no protesters were outside. Only their garbage remained as evidence of the mass that had been there the day before.

Jordan, with Rigo, Davic, Remy, and a handful of PPS agents, chatted with members of the British Columbia delegation - many of whom she was friendly with from her time in the Legislature in Victoria - while waiting for the Chinese, who were running late. Their meeting would concern softwood lumber exports.

The conference room door burst open and a flood of screaming French preceded President Delacroix, who stormed toward Jordan.

Davic moved in front of her, tucking away his BlackBerry, followed by two PPS officers.

"Can I help you, Mr. President?"

Davic caught only brief snippets through the president's foreign tirade, one of which was "connasse Premier LaSalle."

Secret Service agents hurried into the room, after searching the center for the president and only finding him because of his screaming. One of them was politically astute enough to close the door to the conference room.

Remy pulled Jordan farther behind Davic, who kept trying to get the president to speak English and explain what had happened.

"The Québec press are reporting that I drugged and raped *you* at the White House!" Delacroix finally got out.

Davic was stunned, looking at the president like a deer in headlights. The others in the conference room were silenced and stilled. Davic turned to the BC delegation and ordered them out, then turned on the flat-screen TV on the wall. Beau directed him to Ici Radio-Canada Télé: There was a report in French featuring pictures of the Canadians arriving at the White House, Beau and Davic shaking hands, then screenshots of an email.

"They're saying they received an anonymous tip that while *you* were at the White House, *I* drugged and raped you."

"Jesus Christ," Davic mumbled.

Delacroix seized Davic by the collar.

"Did you tell them anything, you little shit?"

"President—"

"How do they know?"

The Secret Service pulled Delacroix and Davic apart and kept them apart.

"Beau!" Jordan cried out. "They obviously *don't* know what happened! They're saying it was *you*, not *Queenie*. We've all heard these conspiracy theories before."

"Why is it headline news *this time*?" Delacroix growled.

Jordan was at a loss now.

"President Delacroix, we had an issue yesterday," Davic began slowly, unsurely.

He spelled out the events, Beau's anger dying down.

"I think this news is another piece in their game," Davic said.

"Whose? Who are they?"

"We're investigating. At the moment we're leaning toward LaSalle or some fringe group with his same ideology. We sent the drawing to CSIS, we could use the CIA's help too."

Beau thought, trying to filter his emotions from his senses.

"Fine, I'll have someone get in contact with you," he said.

Davic extended his hand and Beau sneered at it briefly, then took it.

"Don't fuck with me," he whispered to Davic. "I will destroy you."

He left and Davic was quick to interpret his meaning: If the US pulled out of the trade agreement Beau and Jordan had worked out, it would be a noose around the Canadian economy's neck. Then LaSalle would berate her administration for becoming too reliant on the Americans, the members of Parliament from Québec would pull their support from Jordan, and she would be left in a minority government, at risk of having her administration dissolved and a new election called.

The Chinese delegation started filtering in and Davic compartmentalized these thoughts and started remembering the goals for this meeting.

Davic was heading back to the conference after lunch. His head was down, looking at his phone, and caught a glimpse of shoes in front of him. Looking up he saw Nigella, in a beautiful red summer dress with a pair of tan heels. She was smiling at him and it made all of Davic's anxiety from the past 12 hours fall away and all he had in his head was her.

"Can I steal you for a bit?" she asked.

He offered no resistance as she pulled him into an empty meeting room, where she sat him in a chair, then sat in his lap, facing him. This close, she could see the texture of the cover-up over one eye and when she rubbed at it, Davic winced and pulled away, though she had gotten enough removed to see that he was covering up a bruise.

"What happened?"

"I fell down some stairs at the hotel," Davic quickly explained. "You might have noticed I'm not the most attentive."

"Is that why you canceled last night?"

"Yeah."

"Are you telling me the truth?" she asked, running a hand through his hair.

"Of course."

"You didn't get into a fist fight with the Black Spy?"

Davic was momentarily mystified by this, then recalled the *Spy vs. Spy* comic in *Mad Magazine*. As Nigella's hand ran down his neck, then chest, he understood what she was going for.

"Fine...You caught me. The Black Spy cornered me in an alley. He had a gun. I wrestled it away from him but he caught me with his elbow."

Nigella smiled, pressing herself harder against him as Davic wrapped an arm around her waist and squeezed.

"Give me names, details," she said, pulling on his tie.

"I don't know his name but he's CIA, Special Ops. He wants to kill me but he doesn't know who he's messing with."

"Oh, *Agent Q*," Nigella gushed, chuckling, and she leaned in for a kiss.

Davic's phone, in his pocket, buzzed with an alarm and both he and Nigella jumped at the feeling.

Another meeting was starting soon. He stood, both hands still on Nigella, whom he gave several deeper kisses.

"I have to get outta here," he said.

"I want a full report. *Tonight*."

"I promise you a full *debriefing*."

Nigella smirked, then Davic exited the empty room.

That evening Davic went to Nigella's room, flowers in hand, ready to take her to the receptions and political social events for the evening. Nigella instead answered the door wearing only heels and one of her fancy hats. She grabbed Davic by his tie and pulled him into her room. Davic held out the flowers, not sure what to do or say.

"How sweet," Nigella said, taking the flowers and setting them aside. "Now, need to strip search you; make sure you're not wearing a wire."

Davic grinned.

"Spread'em," she barked and Davic compiled, letting Nigella feel him up. She removed his jacket and continued checking Davic. She pressed her warm body against him as she worked on the buttons of his waistcoat. "What are you hiding?"

"Nothing," Davic replied, leaning down for a kiss.

"Trying to distract me with your masculine wiles?"

In the morning in Nigella's room, Davic woke up with the sun. He watched her sleep for a little bit. He was already thinking of living with her in London. They had been dating for about six months now - "dating" the nearest equivalent to the long-distance relationship necessary for their stations in life.

Once Jordan's time as Prime Minister was done - however long that would be - he intended to request a position at the London Embassy.

But maybe he was just being foolish thinking that way, the term "puppy dog" love occurring to him. Nigella was the first substantial romantic relationship he'd had and he wasn't ignorant of the fact that many people fall "head over heels" in love, start immediately planning their whole lives around the other person.

How long could it really last? There were many things

Nigella didn't know about him, and maybe never would. She didn't know about his childhood, she didn't know about his brain damage, she didn't know the scars on his wrist hadn't come from a machine accident on his grandparents' farm - as he'd told her.

Davic had initially told her the scars had come from the Russians handcuffing and interrogating him once he'd been found out as a spy in Russia. And the dent under his rib cage? That had come from being shot by an FSB officer - how could he tell her the truth, that it had come from his feeding tube when he'd been in the hospital after whatever had happened to fuck up his memory? How could he tell her the truth, that there was a part of his life that was a complete blank?

Nigella liked the excitement that came along with the illusion that he was some sort of spy, but she had to know she was kidding herself. They both knew Davic was just a computer nerd playing a political professional. Soon the shine would wear off and she would be on her way to another fling.

Maybe, if he could fill in that blank spot, then he could think about his life, a relationship, long-term. Davic needed to know who he was before he could share that with another person. But with the recent threats to Jordan's administration, and only the scantest of leads to follow, he couldn't hold out hope. He needed to focus on protecting Jordan.

Nigella woke shortly after he'd started the shower and she got in with him. They washed each other's hair and bodies, lingering over the other's chest and hips. She pressed herself in close and pulled his head down gently, urging him to kiss her, and he did.

"I love you," Nigella whispered.

David froze, looking down into her face, anxious, hopeful, searching. He wanted to say it back to her, but his vocal chords were twisted. So instead he wrapped his arms around her and hugged her tightly.

Davic and Nigella had breakfast with Basil and Smyth that morning in Basil's room.

Nigella, thus far, had not revealed anything of interest about Davic to Basil, though Basil was not yet ready to write Davic off as purely what he played himself. He may very well be the type to keep things from even those closest to him - Jordan included.

Still, Nigella, despite her reputation as a tart, was not a dumb girl. Throughout his time as Prime Minister, she had always been perspicacious enough to tell when something was bothering her father, even when the only other person he'd confided in was Smyth. If Nigella suspected something amiss with Davic's activities, she would badger it out of him. Aside from the fact they could not spend as much time together as they wanted, Nigella had had no complaints about their relationship, which now outdistanced any of her other relationships by leaps and bounds.

"How did you come by the name 'Davic?'" Basil asked as they ate.

"My dad. My mom wanted to call me Hadrian."

"Fine name. What do your parents do?"

Basil knew the answer already, from Davic's file - his parents were dead and he'd been adopted at 15 by Cy Drew. And Basil would not put it past Davic's intelligence to know that Basil knew this. But he wanted to see if Davic might deviate from what his file said.

He didn't but there was a new development: Nigella hadn't known Davic's parents died when he was six. So he did keep information about himself secret.

Nigella was sad and stroked Davic's shoulder, even as he assured her it was not necessary.

Throughout the breakfast Davic got the impression all this talk was an interrogation veiled under a cloak of amiability. Basil so far had had no objections to Davic's relationship with his daughter, though this may have changed if Beau Delacroix had gotten the Prime Minister's ear and voiced his suspicions that it was Davic who had leaked to the Québec media.

After the food was finished, Nigella excused herself to finish getting ready for the day's events. Once the three men were alone, Davic quickly understood this was what Basil had invited them to breakfast for in the first place.

"What you reveal here with us now will not leave this room," Basil began.

His eyes bore into Davic's, he could almost feel them drilling into his brain.

"What happened at the White House?"

Word of Beau's outburst had spread from the BC delegation and gotten to Smyth. Davic told them the truth, as much as he could remember, then supplemented it with Rigo's attempted kidnapping.

"We have some friends in the French delegation," Basil said. "We'll ask them to talk with LaSalle, try to keep his head screwed on, and keep your boss' friends in Parliament happy."

"And send me the picture," Smyth said. "We'll run it through MI6."

"And Nigella is not to know of any of this."

"Of course," Davic said.

Back at the convention center, the Canadians headed for a meeting with the Americans. Nigella had applied more cover-up to Davic's eyes on the drive over. Smyth accompanied Basil and them into one wing of the center, then Basil went to speak with some of the French delegation while Smyth remained near the entrance and Nigella went with Davic toward a coffee and sandwich bar along one wall.

Davic kept an eye on his watch, wanting to arrive at the

meeting just in time for it to begin, the better to prevent Delacroix from blowing up again.

He got a call from an unsaved number and when he answered it, he could hear a voice speaking as though from the bottom of a well. Plugging one ear did not help, the reception area was too loud.

"I'll be right back," he said, moving around Nigella, then turning into a short hallway, where he found a door to a stairwell, which he entered.

Ten minutes into the meeting, Davic still had not come into the conference room. Jordan texted him, 'Where are you?' but received no reply - unusual for Davic, who usually responded in seconds.

Nigella had wandered over beside her father to help charm the French delegates into keeping LaSalle in line.

Smyth, from his position beside the entrance, looked over the people in the reception area: Everything seemed to be going all right.

But where was Davic?

His tall blond head should have been easy to find but after several scans, Smyth could not find him. He was able to pull Nigella away from her father without drawing the attention of the delegates and after she told him she'd last seen Davic go into the stairwell to take a phone call, Smyth hurried across the reception area to the short corridor.

The opening of the door echoed throughout the cement stairwell, which was otherwise silent, not a whisper of Davic's voice.

"Davic Woods?"

Seconds went by and no response.

Smyth's suspicions were instantly aroused, given the events Davic had told them about in the last few days. He went to the security booth, showed them his credentials, and asked to see the camera feed in the stairwell. A guard switched one of the screens over but it was black.

"What the hell?" the guard grumbled.

Smyth left the booth and headed back to the entrance, saying into his radio:

"All units, be on the lookout, we have a missing person: Davic Woods, 6'2", blond, converge on all the northern entrances..."

Chapter 10: To Turn Again

The doctors had no way of knowing how Davic would respond once they brought him out of his coma. He may be in a permanent fugue state, or temporary, he may have lost the ability to speak, to understand, he may be delusional.

They stressed this all to Cy while they waited for the barbiturates to exit his system enough to allow his heart rate to increase and his brain functions to restart.

In the beginning he was lethargic and confused. His motor functions, reflexes, and feeling seemed to be normal. He was taken off the feeding tube and was put on a liquid diet.

Cy brought Davic the framed picture of his family - what had always been his most prized possession. But when he showed it to Davic, there was no response.

For several days he lay almost perfectly still on one side, facing the wall. Cy stayed with him, talking to him, reading to him, and holding his hand or rubbing his back.

Then he started speaking, answering the nurse's assessment questions: Who was the Prime Minister, what year was it, what was his own name?

His responses were slow but accurate. When Cy showed Davic the framed picture again, he cried.

After a month, he was determined to be in no physical peril anymore and was discharged into the care of an in-patient brain-injury rehab facility, to which Cy flew him.

His long-term memory seemed fine - he remembered the names of his parents, grandparents, and foster parents, his coworkers at CSIS.

The UK was where his memories started fading.

"Where did you work in the UK?" Cy asked.

Davic struggled to think.

"I...I don't know."

"You went somewhere with some people after the UK. Do you remember any of that?"

Davic teared up, frustrated, shook his head.

"Where did I go?"

Cy sidestepped his questions with more questions of his own.

As the weeks went by, it became clear that Davic had no memories of Afghanistan and only the spottiest memories of GCHQ and the UK. In addition, his short-term memory, his memory-making and storing abilities, were touch and go.

Some mornings the nurse, the same as from the day before and the day before that, would have to remind Davic of her name. And sometimes, when Cy asked if he remembered what he'd had for lunch the day before - smoothies with various ingredients morning, noon, and night for the first two weeks after he woke up - Davic couldn't say.

His higher-thinking skills were tested once a week by a psychologist with games like Tic-Tac-Toe and Connect-4, then he was quizzed on concepts and terminology from his computer-science textbooks: What differentiated Java from JavaScript? What were the primary components of an effective cybersecurity system?

The psychologist didn't understand Davic's responses but was evaluating the flow with which Davic spoke, the confidence, the quickness with which he responded, and with these criteria, the psychologist concluded that what Davic was saying was true, was knowledge he'd previously encoded and was retrieving successfully.

Cy had to miss a lot of work and gave as few details to his director and Thor as possible. All the director learned was that Davic had been involved in an accident while on exchange with GCHQ. When he realized the file had been sealed and he could get no further information, he pried Cy for more, but Cy was a fortress.

Smyth had already seen about erasing any record of Davic's time in GCHQ. Now Cy requested Davic's position be dissolved.

"Why?" the director asked in shock. "You said he was recovering."

Cy could tell the director was loath to lose Davic solely for the reason that he was good with Viking and Thor valued him. But Cy declined to elaborate and finally the director signed off on the revocation of Davic's credentials.

"You explain this to Thor," the director said before signing and Cy understood this was quid-pro-quo.

And Cy did, in a private meeting with Thor.

"Does he still have all his faculties?" Thor asked.

"Yes."

Thor looked pensive for a moment.

"Something happened," Thor said after a while. "Something terrible."

Cy breathed in and out slowly.

"Yes."

"Removing him from here protects him."

"Yes."

Thor nodded.

"Your son is brilliant," Thor said. "When brilliant people don't work at what they love, they become miserable. When he's ready, let him know he always has a place in the Viking family no matter what."

Chapter 11: Questioning the Void

Davic was unconscious, naked down to his boxers, and handcuffed to a metal folding chair, his ankles tied with rope. His scars suggested he had been in a similar situation before, more severe bindings previously cutting into his flesh. He was in some sort of industrial building, abandoned, chunks of concrete and dirt piled around, rusted rebar. An LED work light stood across from him, washing him in its radiance.

Two black-clothed masked figures stepped into the light and moved beside Davic. One was tall and bulky, the second short and slight, pulling a rattling metal cart on which was a polygraph monitor attached to a laptop. The smaller figure wrapped the body sensors, or pneumographs, around Davic's torso, then cinched two smaller circular sensors, galvanometers, around the ring and index finger on Davic's right hand, and finally the blood-pressure cuff around Davic's left bicep. She turned on the machine and when the low humming sounded, the larger figure broke open a caged-in pair of smelling salts and waved them under Davic's nostrils.

Davic woke up with a sharp intake of air, reddened eyes opening wide, and it took him a moment to come to his senses and observe his surroundings. Then he saw the two masked figures, the familiarity of whom ignited his anger.

"Where am I?"

The smaller figure was attending to the machine Davic recognized as a polygraph.

"Would you like a glass of water?" the larger figure asked.

"I wanna know who you are."

The larger figure turned to the polygraph tech.

"Ready?"

"Yeah," the tech said.

The graph on the computer started scrolling, lines level. The larger figure turned back to Davic.

"Is your name Davic Woods?"

Davic glared up at the eyes peering out of the balaclava.

"You one of the guys that tried to kidnap Rigo?" Davic asked.

The figure was silent.

"Mr. Woods, cooperate or things will get *much* worse."

Davic clenched his fists.

"Is your name Davic Woods?" the figure asked again.

"Yes."

"Are you a former CSIS technical analyst?"

"...Yes."

"Did you enjoy your job?"

"...Yes."

"You were relieved of that position for reasons unknown to you?"

"*Yes.*"

A spike in the lines on the computer screen.

"You were angry when you were released from that position?"

"...Yes."

"Are you a member of any insurrectionist, separatist, or terrorist group?"

This was a sharp turnoff from where Davic had seen the interrogation going.

"No."

"Is Jordan Innis a member of any insurrectionist, separatist, or terrorist group?"

"*No.*"

"Have you ever used sensitive information you obtained through your political position as a way to blackmail or otherwise profit from somebody in a position of power?"

Davic hesitated for only a second - he couldn't say for

sure he *hadn't*, even just working with the party whip to make sure the MPs showed up for votes could be seen as something akin to blackmail - but why was he even concerned about telling the truth to these people, whoever they were?

"No."

The large figure saw the lines on the computer spike only a little.

"Has Jordan Innis ever used sensitive information obtained—"

"For fuck's sake, *no!*"

"—through her political position as a way to blackmail or otherwise profit from somebody in a position of power?"

"No!"

"Have you ever plotted someone's kidnapping?"

"No."

"Have you ever plotted someone's murder?"

"No."

"Did the President of the United States drug and rape you?"

"No."

"Did the first lady of the United States drug and rape you?"

Hesitated.

"No."

The lines remained level.

The larger figure was silent for a moment. Obviously he wasn't getting the responses he wanted.

"Did you give the Québecers any privileged information about the President and first lady of the United States?"

"No."

The figure did not follow up with another question immediately. The larger figure went beside the polygraph tech and Davic could hear only whispering. Finally the larger figure came in front of Davic again and removed his mask.

"My name is John Bowser, I'm with the CIA."

Davic's mind hurriedly put the pieces together.

"Delacroix told me the CIA would help investigate our issue, so you kidnap and interrogate *me*?"

"Our plant overheard you talking with Nigella Thatcher," Bowser said.

"When?"

"Yesterday," Bowser said, picking up a transcript from the polygraph cart. "'The Black Spy is CIA, Special Ops, he wants to kill me but I'm gonna kill him.' Ring a bell?"

"Yeah."

"How do you explain it?"

"I was trying to turn on my girlfriend."

"You weren't sending a message?"

"To who?"

"The agent we had tailing you. He is, as you say, a 'Black spy.'"

Davic took a second to make the connection. Then he started laughing.

"You dumb bastard," he said. "Even an intelligence agency isn't immune to the stupidity of its boss."

Bowser wanted to hit him, Davic could tell, even though he couldn't stop laughing at the buffoon. Bowser and the polygraph tech headed around a corner, and a few seconds later, Davic heard a door open, saw sunlight pour in, then close.

In addition to Davic's absence, Smyth also noted he hadn't seen Beau Delacroix's head of security, a former CIA operator, John Bowser. Realizing this he wanted to find Bowser himself, use a pair of pliers on his toenails until he told Smyth where Davic was and what he'd taken him for.

But Smyth remembered the consequences of impulsive decisions he'd made in his life: Because of Delacroix's volatile nature, any inkling of the UK and the US working against each other would threaten the relationship they had.

Besides Basil, it was unlikely Smyth had the ability to scare Delacroix, Bowser's puppet master. So, before the UK's second round of trade negotiations - this one with the US - Smyth told Basil that Bowser was missing too. And as it had been for Smyth, this was too much of a coincidence.

As an American functionary was talking about the benefits of the proposed changes in trade policy, Basil moved beside Delacroix. Smyth had been able to keep Nigella and the Canadians calm, in the dark, so far as to Davic's absence by saying he was in a phone conference between CSIS and MI6. But it had already been two hours and soon they would take no more assurances until they saw Davic in the flesh.

"Where's your CIA lackey?" Basil asked lowly. In his peripheral vision, Basil saw Beau smirk smugly.

"We ain't talking spy stuff today."

"But we should. Because while you're occupied with twisting your allies' arms, our enemy is busy planning their next attack."

Beau didn't respond.

"Davic is a steel trap when it comes to sensitive information," Basil said. "He and Jordan Innis, if they are...*questionable,* are master manipulators. Davic would not leak information about whatever happened at the White House to the press just to embarrass you. If anything, he would store it away for future use, for material benefit."

"So you admit they are pulling strings," Beau said.

"Don't we all? " Basil asked. "Whether the strings they're pulling are detrimental to us remains to be seen. For now I'm more concerned with finding the people responsible for trying to kidnap Rigo Barbossa. It is a dangerous precedent for family and friends of world leaders to be taken. And right now, with Davic and Bowser missing, it doesn't look good for *you.*"

"Is that a threat?"

"A gentle nudging. Return Davic to the hotel and no one will be any the wiser."

"Or what?"

"If you hinder our investigation into finding the would-be kidnappers by terrorizing our friends because of superficial grievances, you pose a risk to me. And as a risk, it would materially benefit me to get you out of office as quickly as possible. What does *Quentin* call the drink she used to incapacitate Davic? A *Stud Rider*?"

Beau's anger caused his body to go rigid. He looked over at Basil and could see the killer animal just beneath the British Prime Minister's aristocratic veneer. He knew Basil was not above confirming the fake news report if it served his purpose. Twisting of news and perception had long been a political tool.

Stiffly, Beau stood and took out his cell phone as he stepped out of the conference room.

Davic was clothed and Bowser put a hood over his head before leading him out of the abandoned building, into a vehicle, then he was driven for maybe 15 minutes before he was deposited in an alleyway. The car was gone before he could get the hood removed and make it to the sidewalk.

There were texts and voicemails from the Canadians and the Brits. One was from Smyth telling him, once he was released, to call only Smyth, which he did, and sent him his GPS location. Then he waited to be picked up by one of Smyth's officers.

Chapter 12: Redemption is Innis All

Prior to being discharged from the rehab in Victoria, Davic had tried to get his life back in Ottawa in order for his return. Since coming to the rehab, he'd told anyone who would listen how he was looking forward to getting well enough to return to his job - though he didn't tell anyone where he worked, just it was computer related.

He talked to Cy most nights and asked him how it was going at CSIS.

Finally, a week before he was going to be discharged, Cy broke the news:

"CSIS has rescinded your employment, Dav."

The words were so alien to Davic, he thought they may have been a delusion from his brain injury.

"Why?"

"They consider you a risk," Cy said. "It's policy that no one with any kind of brain trauma be allowed to handle intelligence."

"But...I'm getting better."

"But on your hospital papers, it says 'traumatic brain injury.' It's stupid but CSIS is strict on this."

"I don't even remember what happened! Why is that being used against me?"

"It's supposed to *protect* you, Davic. If any information got out and there was an incident - officers or soldiers died - who do you think most people would blame? The guy with a brain injury."

Davic couldn't believe it but the fact was the CSIS chapter of his life was over. Cy got him a plane ticket back to Ottawa for the morning after he was discharged.

They didn't talk about what would or could happen

next. Cy didn't want to overwhelm Davic with too many thoughts of the future. Davic did have the offer from Viking, but for now Cy just wanted him home where he was safe and they would figure it out from there.

After he was discharged, Davic was driven by one of the rehab vans to the hotel he would stay at until his flight. But immediately upon arriving there, he called a cab and took himself to a beach near Sooke.

It was a beautiful summer day. Down in the sand Davic spread out a blanket and ate the food he'd brought, not tasting it, just wanting the extra weight it would add to his gut.

He'd broken the SIM card from his phone and turned off the location detection.

He'd arrived during the morning swell, when the beach was heavy with families. In a few hours, as the riptide strengthened, the people went off, leaving him alone, at least along this strip of the beach, which was all he needed.

The doctors at the rehab had called his current state of mind anhedonia - he felt no pleasure or positive emotions and couldn't imagine he ever would again.

But had he ever, for that matter?

When he'd graduated early with his degrees, he'd only gotten a stronger sense of purpose. Everything had only been stepping stones to get where he had no idea he wanted to be: at CSIS, using his skills to help keep people safe.

But now that was gone. And probably his open job offer at Viking was gone too. If word got out that a security-technology manufacturer had hired a brain-damaged tech, it would likely degrade clients' - the FVEY's - trust in the technology.

But then he didn't really care, at least about not being able to work at Viking. It had never appealed to him, and even if they were to hire him, it would just be a job, something he could never love.

At CSIS he could see for himself whether the people he was monitoring were good or bad and adjust his supervision accordingly. At Viking he would just be part of the manufacturing process to create the technology that other people, many without his same ethics, could use to monitor people as they saw fit.

Intelligence and security technology, as with many things, were tools that could be used for good just as much as evil. It all hinged on the operator, and if he could not be that operator, then what purpose did he have?

He was sure other agencies in FVEY had the same policy as CSIS - no employees with brain trauma. So what other choices did he have?

His family was dead, he had no friends, and the idea of going through this world merely as a cog in the machine, manufacturing and consuming, was like an anchor around his heart.

He had a backpack with him, full of stuff for Mr. Drew - pictures of them together, and Lemma, books, letters he'd written in the hospital and rehab, and Davic's picture of his family at Christmas. He took this out to look at one last time, then he stood and waded into the cold water, moved deeper and deeper.

Not far off shore, a pod of orca breached, spewing water. Davic, his feet just barely still on the seafloor, watched them and wondered if these would be the first to eat his corpse.

He continued moving, the seafloor dipping below the reach of his feet, and he flailed in the water, not knowing how to swim, and he pumped his legs and swung his arms to push himself farther onward. But the bodily strain quickly caught up with him and caused his muscles to burn, then lose feeling, and he couldn't manipulate them as well. In a minute he was stagnant, submerged, looking up at the unattainable surface.

This was it. And whether it was the anhedonia or not,

his last thought was that this was where he belonged now.

Jordan was in a kayak with another woman and in the split second of looking over to one side as she dipped the paddle, she saw the refracted form of a human body maybe 15 feet below.

Jordan stood in her cockpit and tore off her lifejacket, then dove into the water. She sailed down as naturally as a fish, found Davic, whose face was pale, his lips blue, and pulled him back to the surface, where her companion in the twin-hull kayak tried to keep the boats stable to allow Jordan to throw Davic across the decks without capsizing the vessels.

Jordan pulled herself on top, then knelt beside Davic, pumping his chest and respiring into his mouth.

Finally a spasm racked Davic's body and he vomited water and both women tried to keep him as still as possible, lest his panic tip the kayak. Jordan stroked his hair and face, soothing him, telling him her name, where he was, he was OK.

Immediately Davic was filled with the strongest anger he'd ever felt: Why would these complete fucking strangers stop him, what fucking right did they have, how could they possibly think they were helping, would it help them sleep better at night, were they hoping to get their names in the papers, be awarded medals or commended by their clergy, reserve a spot in heaven? *Why couldn't they just mind their own business?*

They paddled back to the beach and Davic found he hadn't drifted too far away from his morbid picnic, and his anger extinguished as quickly as a lit match under a waterfall: He'd tried to kill himself. He hadn't been able to name the act prior to attempting it, maybe because calling it suicide was ludicrous. Davic would never kill himself! But what fucking else had he been trying to do, train to become an Olympic breath-holder?

The women, though, didn't notice the sparse spread, not immediately. They wanted to take him to the hospital.

"No, *please*, I'm all right," Davic urged them, imagining a permanent residency in a mental ward would be the end result and the thought of Mr. Drew being informed of this, after all he'd already been through with Davic, was too painful to think much about.

What would Mr. Drew think? What would his father think? They wouldn't recognize him, no way this could be the same Davic Mr. Drew knew, nor the Davic his father had hoped his son would become. He thought about the words scrawled by his father on the back of the Christmas picture: "Be brave, be strong, be good."

And with this one act, Davic had failed on all three counts, his father's final thoughts, his last message to his son as he slowly died. His cowardice and his weakness and his utter failure mixed and it felt as though the resulting toxic concoction replaced his blood. As it coursed through him, he started crying in front of these strangers.

"What happened?" Jordan asked, unsurely reaching for Davic, hesitating, but then still going to rub his back.

When that didn't help, all Jordan could think to do was hug him and Davic tentatively hugged her back, his arms at first loose around her abdomen, then tightening as his sadness reached repeated highs.

Once he'd expelled some of the pent-up emotion, his reason returned to remind him of the very likely possibility that these women would call an ambulance and take him to the hospital. He composed himself, apologized, and tried to think of a plausible explanation, anything but the truth, but he came up blank.

Jordan, prior to Davic's breakdown, had been thinking that somehow, even after years of kayaking, she had somehow not seen Davic in the water and driven the kayak straight into him, though he didn't have wounds or blood spilled. Now it was clear Davic had been driven into the water by some emotional distress. It was remarkable to see such emotion, such reality, raw despair, come from such a handsome young man. Jordan found she still had a hand on Davic's shoulder long after he'd gotten himself back together.

The other woman was looking around, perhaps for help, perhaps to see if they'd attracted any attention, and in so doing, she spotted the blanket and the backpack across the beach.

"Is that yours?" she asked Davic.

Davic looked to where she pointed and the sight immediately struck him as utterly sad. Then he looked at it from an objective perspective: What a sad scene, a picnic with just enough food for one.

Inspiration suddenly struck and he looked back at Jordan.

"I had a date," he said with all the confidence of a theatre actor performing for a non-English-speaking audience. "She...didn't show up."

It was flimsy but he hoped the emotional aspect of the story would conceal its warts.

They gathered up his blanket and backpack, then took him to Jordan's car. After getting him out of his clothes - a suit, expensive, Jordan saw on the label, another questionable element of this scenario, which made Jordan think harder – they wrapped him in towels and sat him in the passenger seat with the heat on. And Davic did not fail to notice Jordan's brow crinkle as she took his jacket and threw it over the hood of the car.

After looking around and not finding it, Jordan's companion asked where Davic's car was.

With a foundation set and some time to think now, Davic started to clean up his story.

"I was hoping to get engaged today," he said. "You can probably guess what she said."

Jordan's companion responded with a mewling sound,

as though she'd just watched a touching scene in a romance movie. Jordan was silent, rubbing his shoulder.

Jordan was a backbench member of the British Columbia Legislative Assembly, which she revealed after she and Davic discovered they had both seen the same pod of orca, and Jordan was working on legislation to protect the local population.

She was also the owner of a kayaking business and today she'd been out on a lesson, her companion the student. They had come to the beach to practice dealing with rip tides.

The three drove in Jordan's car to her storefront in Sooke, where the student took her own car home.

"Do you live around here?" Jordan asked then.

Davic had already composed a response to this predicted question.

"I'm here on business. I'm at a hotel in Victoria."

This stirred the pot of suspicion in Jordan's brain.

"I thought you were here to propose to your girlfriend."

"Yeah," Davic replied automatically, taking a second to expound. "She lives here. I come here often."

"Where do you work?"

"You'll need a password to access that file."

Jordan smirked, thinking, her fingers rapping her steering wheel.

"I don't think you should be alone tonight," she said.

The young man was obviously exhausted from the day's events and so harmless-looking. If it came to it, for whatever reason, Jordan was sure she could handle Davic. Her kayak weighed more than he did soaking wet.

Davic was inclined to protest, to insist that he was all right, and just wanted to go back to the hotel to sleep. But he knew there was an unspoken ultimatum here: either Jordan's apartment or the hospital.

Jordan was gently assertive, offering Davic something to drink and eat, if he would like, when they entered, then continuing conversation - telling Davic about her work so far in the legislature, asking Davic about his life, which required quite a bit of mental acrobatics on Davic's part in order to come up with answers that wouldn't give away too much - as she sat on the couch. Davic, never well versed in social etiquette, had nowhere to retreat to, so was obliged to sit on the other side of the couch.

He was amazed that, after a grueling hour, suddenly he felt a release of the tension throughout his body. It was as though Davic's instincts had run a deep background check of its own on Jordan and gave to Davic's brain a report saying she was trustworthy.

After the onset of this feeling, Davic's stomach groaned, the first time he could remember since before the hospital. Jordan got from the kitchen a bowl of figs and put on the kettle for tea, then heated up some meatloaf.

Davic now engaged her in conversation, asking about her interest in politics, her hopes.

"It sounds cliché but I wanna make the world a better place," she said. "Granted, what people define as 'better' differs greatly."

"I think we need smaller government. Government isn't meant to be a Snuggie - one size shouldn't fit all."

Jordan snickered.

Politics had never been a big part of his job, but Davic had long been exposed to threats created by politics and these surely had left impressions on him that he used to formulate opinions. It felt strange to voice these, but he wanted to keep talking with Jordan.

"I agree. Government's a necessary evil," she said. "It's not there to replace family and community."

Jordan, with other new acquaintances, had always been conscious to mind what she said politically, the topic being such an inherently divisive topic. Because of this she'd become used to a certain apprehension in meeting and talking with unknown people, especially as it related to her job. But with Davic there was none of that apprehension, hadn't been any since she pulled him out of the ocean. Though she didn't know what his job was, she sensed it was something that shielded him, in a way, from the ugliness of politics. He was awkward, thought a little too long about what he would say before saying it, and had a way of strangely articulating statements and questions, but all of these qualities endeared him to Jordan, gained him her trust, quicker than she could believe.

"Do you know about identity politics? The concept of equity over equality?" Davic asked.

"Boy, do I! Those are some of the biggest threats to western culture, I think," Jordan said.

Davic found himself talking about himself, telling the truth as much as he could. He told her he had worked for CSIS but had been let go, he didn't know why. He wanted to tell her more, tell her where he'd been for the last two months and why, and why he'd really gone to the beach that day but that was too much, his voice froze before he could utter a word of this.

Jordan silently seemed to understand that getting any information out of a CSIS staffer was a small miracle and did not push to know more. She asked if he would go back to Ottawa.

"I don't know," Davic said, truly wondering himself.

Jordan nodded, quiet for a beat.

"You can stay here for as long as you want," she said.

The offer made Davic want to explode with excitement, anxiety, a dozen emotions, but most of all desire. Being so near Jordan for an indefinite amount of time made Davic want to touch her, hold her, kiss her. He'd never felt like this before but now, looking at Jordan, his heart beat so fast, it felt like it would explode. He wanted to blurt out he loved her - if he didn't do it spontaneously, there was no way he could - but his rational mind squeezed his vocal chords, preventing him.

Just a few hours ago, he'd been defeated and had tried to kill himself, the failure of which had led to an even worse feeling, and he'd been more exhausted than ever. Now, just talking with Jordan had reinvigorated him. He had in him a font of energy he had no idea what to do with - he had impulses to pull Jordan to her feet and dance with her, to run with her around the neighborhood of her apartment.

Was this what people felt before they had sex? Is that what he wanted? But what about Jordan? He'd never understood body language, if she was saying something nonverbally to him, he wasn't picking up on it. He wanted to kiss her, to feel her, but he didn't want to alienate her, he didn't want to be thrown out of her apartment, her life. But what if she wanted him to "make a move," whatever the hell that meant? Would she hate him if he didn't do something when she wanted him to?

He felt like there were fire ants crawling all over him, biting him. The situation was impossible to exist in and with the same abandon he'd gone into ocean to kill himself, Davic reached across the couch, cupped her cheek, and tried to move in for a kiss but his shame stepped on him like an ant and ground his impulse to death.

But Jordan didn't pull away and with him already bridging the gap in between them on the couch, she leaned in and locked him in a kiss.

Did she believe Davic's story of a failed proposal? She wasn't sure. But she just wanted to be near to him as possible. It was such a romantic, dramatic story; she wished some prince would lavish such attention on her. If she were a rebound, she would deal with that later, but for now, she just wanted to live in the moment.

They moved closer as though a straitjacket had been wrapped around them both. After kissing for seconds, minutes, or hours, Jordan pulled him up and led him to her bedroom.

In the morning Jordan had to go to her office to attend a session later in the day. As Davic had no other clothes beside the suit he'd come with, Jordan proposed he come to the office with her, then take her car to go buy some new clothes and whatever else he needed.

Davic agreed and Jordan gave him a tour of her office, during which they saw on a staffer apparently on hold on the phone. When Jordan asked who she was calling, the staffer said ICT, her password had randomly reset and she couldn't log into her computer.

Davic asked Jordan if he could try fixing the issue for the staffer, and with her permission he called up the computer's terminal, typed in some code, and the computer logged into the staffer's account.

After Davic left to go shopping, Jordan talked with the office finance manager, asking if they had the budget to hire Davic, perhaps as Jordan's webmaster, a position which had been empty since January. The manager gave her the thumbs-up and later that afternoon, after the session, she asked Davic if would he like the job. At first Davic thought this would be a huge change in his life - he'd have to move to Victoria, explain to Cy why he'd missed his flight - but now that he enumerated the things he'd have to do, it seemed that it wasn't such a big decision. He agreed.

Chapter 13: Spy vs. Spy

Once back at the hotel, Davic texted all those who'd tried to contact him, asking if everything was OK, and told them he'd gotten CSIS, MI6, and CIA to collaborate on finding a profile for the artist's rendering of the French diplomat's son's imposter, which was true: He and Smyth had talked on the phone and the Brit told him that Basil had put the fear of God into Beau and would cooperate with the investigation now.

Turning on the TV, Davic saw the story of President Delacroix's predatory tendencies had spread to English-speaking news. The tipper was still not being named, but the journalist who had received the tip and composed the ensuing story was now talking with English-speaking Canadians, perpetuating the story: The French journalist's name was Gilbert Plonk, of *La sentinelle de Québec*, which had lauded LaSalle's anti-Canadian-American alliance during his campaign, and often ran editorials advocating the secession of French Canada from the English provinces.

"The email you received," the anchor said to Plonk, "mentioned a variety of ways that President Delacroix procures victims."

"Yes."

"For example: The first lady, Queenie, is a cross-dresser, the email said, who, as a man, goes to gay bars, lures them into hotels, where she and the President take advantage of them. The email also accuses the Secret Service, the CIA, and the FBI of having 'sex squads' whose single purpose is the procurement of men for the President. Were any specific names of agents from these agencies mentioned in the email?"

"Yes, but these were removed by our news organization."

"Have you been contacted by any of these agencies?"

"We can't say, we're concerned for our safety."

Davic called Smyth again, asked if he'd seen the news, and gave him Plonk's name when he said no. Perhaps a background check on Plonk and his associates could make identifying the man in the artist's rendering easier.

"Tell the CIA and SIS to keep themselves in line," Davic said. "If this guy's part of the group, they wouldn't put him out in the spotlight without a reason. He may be bait to draw our guys into some kind of trap."

After an hour Bowser called him.

"You need to go on the news and defend the President," he said.

Davic had been hoping to avoid this, as it would only give the conspiracy theorists more fuel to feed their fire. Regarding the other conspiracies that surrounded Delacroix's presidency - namely, that he was gay, Queenie was a stand-in or a cross-dresser - no one from his administration had spoken to the news, though surely some must have known the truth - which, to Davic, meant Bowser had, in one way or another, taken care of those who had left the administration.

But this conspiracy was different and Davic knew he had to oblige, to keep peace with Delacroix, to keep Jordan's reputation safe, and to ensure the best resources were available to find the kidnappers.

He arranged a press conference in a conference room in Toronto's Federal Building at 11 a.m. the next day. By the afternoon of the day before, the media were already reporting on it, speculating as to what Davic would say and how it would affect the negotiations at the G20.

He stayed in his room all that day, talking with Smyth, Bowser, and Remy, and bringing in Jordan's press secretaries to come up with talking points.

Nigella came to his room after lunch, at which time

Davic excused the press secretaries, leaving him and Nigella alone.

"Is it true? What they're saying about Delacroix and you?" she asked.

Davic immediately knew not to tell her the truth and this sentiment was backed up when he remembered Basil ordering Nigella remain in the dark.

"Of course not."

"Then why? What's going on?"

"It's...it's all about the negotiations," Davic said. "Someone doesn't like Jordan and Beau being so close, so they're trying to break them up."

"What about what Smyth told me, you're talking with CSIS and MI6 and the CIA?"

"We're trying to figure out who isn't happy. It's politics, that's it."

Nigella scrutinized him even more intensely than Bowser had.

"You're not telling me everything," she said.

"I'm...trying to keep you safe. You don't need to be exposed to all this insanity."

"But you're not letting me in. You're not letting me be part of your life."

"You *are* part of my life."

"Not enough."

"What do you mean, 'not enough?'"

"We haven't talked about what happened yesterday."

"What happened?"

"...You know."

"No, I don't."

"When I said I loved you."

Davic sighed, shutting his eyes, and trying to reorient his thoughts.

"That's what this is about?" he asked.

"It's part of it. How did you feel?"

Davic stammered.

"I don't know."

"Did you feel *anything*?" she asked.

"Yeah."

"Like what?"

"I don't know, Nigella, I really...I can't talk about this right now."

"Why not?"

"Because…"

"*What*?"

"Because I have to focus on my job, I can't let a fling get in the way."

"What, is that all this is to you, a *fling*?"

"What else would it be?"

"I told you I *loved you*, Davic!"

"Yeah, well, you don't. You're in an imaginary world, Nigella."

"With what?"

"I'm not a *spy*, OK? I'm not an Ian Fleming or Robert Ludlum character, I'm just a fucking computer guy! Stop kidding yourself, stop making more of this than it is."

"Do you think I'm some fucking idiot, I really can't tell reality from some role-playing game to have sex with you?"

"If you wanna have sex with me, just…"

"Just what?"

"I don't know."

"I'm not in love with what I think you could be, OK? When I first met you, you couldn't even look me in the eye until I started with the fucking Agent Q shit. It worked for *you*, it gave you confidence to talk to me, so I kept up with it because I wanted you to feel good, I wanted you to keep talking to me. I love *you*, Davic, OK?"

"It's not that simple, Nigella."

"Why not?"

"There are things I can't tell you."

Nigella smirked.

116

"You sound like a spy."

"It's just the way it is. And you're gonna resent me."

"Why?"

"For keeping shit from you."

Nigella growled in frustration, looking around the room, her arms crossed, shaking her head.

"But you don't have to keep shit from Jordan," she said.

This surprised Davic.

"She's my boss," he said.

"Sure," Nigella said, scoffing. "Are you in love with *her*?"

Davic was speechless, unable to move, trying to formulate a coherent thought.

"OK," Nigella said, nodding after several seconds, and left.

Davic wanted to run after her but he had no idea what he would say. There were too many questions he could not answer, for her as well as himself.

He took a deep breath, then called the press secretaries back in.

It was standing-room only in the conference room the next morning. A hundred seats had been laid out and still there was barely enough room for the cameras or for the reporters to write in their pads.

Davic, Jordan, Rigo, Beau, and Queenie stood backstage with their respective security heads, going over notes. At eleven sharp the five went out and the other four took seats at a table while Davic went behind the podium and spoke to the gathered media.

"You'll notice I have a black eye today," Davic began, looking at the journalists gathered behind the podium. "I invite all of you conspiracy theorists to toss in your two cents on that, but the fact is yesterday I was struck by one of the violent protesters that have plagued this occasion. My name is Davic Woods, the same as the media have reported was sexually assaulted by President Delacroix at the White House. Unequivocally, the White House, the Prime Minister's Office, and myself as the supposed victim deny any such thing ever happened. President Delacroix is an ethical politician, a fine leader, a valued ally to our country, and I consider him a friend. The American and Canadian media, in their craving for ratings, are feeding each other on this conspiracy - not the first but certainly the worst. It is no coincidence that these reports come out at the same time as this most important of gatherings takes place. It's also no coincidence that I was struck by the protesters, some of whom are likely responsible for sending out the anonymous tips you and your colleagues swallowed up like a shark swallows a guppy in one gulp. On each occasion I have met them, I have observed the President and the first lady have a loving, committed marriage, which is an integral component in positive leadership for any country. The fact these accusations reportedly came from an anonymous tip is shameful and detrimental to the public's confidence in all of you, who purport yourselves as 'truth seekers.'"

Then Davic was struck by an idea and he went off script, ending his speech with, "Shame on Québec for promoting these lies."

This last statement's spontaneity drew the surprise of Jordan seated beside Davic, and Beau's ire, who nonetheless remained calm and quiet.

Davic then called for questions from the press be directed only at him. These questions were mostly refigurings of: What had happened at the White House? Had Davic ever seen the President and/or first lady act strangely? How would these accusations affect Canada's and America's relationship? And Davic was authoritative in dismissing the accusations, vehement in his praise of President Delacroix, and condemnatory of his accusers, who furnished no evidence of anything - because they know there is nothing to have evidence of.

Jordan was impressed and Delacroix, though visibly angry, said nothing. Davic's responses were being reported on throughout Canada and America within an hour, with LaSalle tweeting a firestorm, bashing Jordan and Delacroix and spreading theories Davic was being strong armed to make that statement.

From here Davic asked the President, Bowser, and Remy to accompany him and Jordan back to their hotel. Once in Jordan's room, Davic explained the plan he'd suddenly come up with while at the podium.

They compiled a list of people who had been there that night at the White House and who had been made privy to the actual events. Once they had the names of both Americans and Canadians made up, copies were made of the list and each put their name next to several of those listed, then next to that, they wrote seemingly random words: MASON AND ROOK, KIMPTON GEORGE, HOMEWOOD SUITES, FAIRMONT, PHOENIX, and so on, none repeating.

At the bottom, they all wrote: "Rigo is going to Washington, D.C., to see a Redskins game with some reporter-friends, possibly meet the first lady, and tour the Monuments with elementary school kids. He's staying at the _____."

Chapter 14: Ambition and Drive

Jordan and Davic didn't sleep together after that first night. Their conversations continued and deepened, and they quickly became each other's most significant relationship in all of their lives, but they never talked about what had happened that first night.

Some at her office mistook Davic for her boyfriend but she corrected them that he was just her roommate, as confused as the other person was disappointed for her.

It had been wonderful. As far as Jordan was concerned, nothing had gone awry or been cause not to continue along that line. But Davic acted so platonically with her, which she loved, but still she couldn't help but think that they could be more.

Davic had the same feelings and thoughts. In the nights following, he would lie awake, thinking about Jordan's door across from his own, imagined standing and going to her. Would she have him? Probably. He just did not know how to go about starting and maintaining a romantic relationship. It took all he had in him to stay there in his own bed.

Jordan was a good person, ambitious. She was sensitive to the needs of her constituents, she was intelligent and pragmatic. If she could scale up her ideas, she would be a boon to the people of Canada and the world. Davic had asked her if she had ever thought about running for Prime Minister. She'd said it was a dream.

"Dreams can't be attained until they're turned into goals," Davic said.

Jordan just shrugged.

"What I'm doing *here* is important," Jordan said. "That's what I want."

"Do you think you could help more people with a

higher office?"

"Doesn't everyone?"

"No. There are politicians who just want higher office to get more power."

"Yeah. They just say they wanna help people."

"They're manipulative."

Jordan nodded.

"With the right management, this country has the resources to be a haven for everyone," she said. "Government should only be a support system to help people reach their full potential. But too many people, both in and out of government, use it to only benefit themselves."

Davic chose his next words carefully.

"Intelligence agencies get the short end of the stick," he said. "When we fuck up, everyone finds out and they hate us, because we're invading their privacy. But when we do our job properly, which is 90 percent of the time, people never find out - and they shouldn't. People deserve to feel safe and *be* safe and that's what I loved about it. I could help with that. But...I got demoted. I could've stayed, taken on a different job, not as an analyst, something menial, low-level, low-clearance. If I couldn't...handle the technology, see the people I was surveilling, be active, then...I didn't wanna have any part of it anymore."

"Why?"

"I didn't wanna work for people who may just be using government to benefit themselves."

Davic wanted her to run for Prime Minister, told her flat-out, a month or so after he'd moved in with her. He would manage the digital campaign and arrange public events. All she had to do was speak from her heart, tell the truth, and never lose sight of their goal - to make the country as hospitable to and safe for its people as possible.

And Davic walked a fine line: He needed to be there, her campaign would need his skills and knowledge, but at the same time, he needed to be as invisible as possible, lest any of Jordan's opponents use his history against her. If knowledge of his time in the hospital became widespread, the title of 'campaign manager' instead of 'boyfriend' would draw less condemnation and criticism as to Jordan's judgment.

Jordan thought Davic was just an optimist, perhaps his failed suicide attempt had jolted his perspective from depression to idealism and he was now trying to create, at least for himself, a world of that latter quality. She thought this until six months later, when Harold Keystone, Premier of British Columbia, asked her to become Deputy Party Leader.

Davic never told her whether he'd had any part in influencing Keystone, with whom Jordan had only ever had the most fleeting of interactions, but she knew he did. How else could she explain this sudden fortune?

Davic had contacted Keystone after a thorough review of BC's media and talking with constituents. The public perception was that Keystone had surrounded himself with "an ol'-boy's club," which Davic convinced him would be a major point of contention when it came to reelection. Davic then had presented Jordan: a backbench MLA, sure, but she had an extensive history of proposing and supporting successful legislation, had won her first and subsequent elections by landslides, and she was a well-liked member of her community, thanks to her kayaking business. She was pretty, straightforward, well-spoken, and could present a fresh face for the party, whose leader's secret Parkinson's was starting to degrade his ability to govern effectively.

At the Party Conference that year in Vancouver, she, Davic, and the Party President talked.

"Your aide and I have been talking about you. I don't think we've ever met but from what he's said, you're very impressive and your new job has been working well for everyone."

"Yeah, I'm enjoying it.

"Between us and the wall, the Federal Party Leader is going to step down at the end of the year," the President said. "I want to propose you as his potential replacement."

Jordan had no doubt that Davic had played a significant role in getting her this opportunity too. As Party Leader, she would be the Prime Minister! The idea was intimidating but turning it down felt like the stupidest thing she could ever do.

"Yes, of course," she said. "I'd be honored."

Throughout the rest of the conference, she and Davic texted back and forth, with most of his messages being encouraging and allaying her fears, assuring her he would be with her every step of the way.

Over dinner that night, Davic finally asked her.

"If...*when* you become PM, I need a favor...a personal favor."

Chapter 15: Where Fools Russian

Davic knew there were holes in his plot. If there were more than one leak, for example, the two might discuss what the President, Prime Minister, Davic, Bowser, or Remy had talked to them about. If that happened, they would realize they had been told different stories about Rigo and detect the deception.

But that was a chance they had to take to rout out the leak.

It had been subtle: The five had talked to each of the people whose names they'd taken on the list and in casual conversation had told them how Rigo would be flying to D.C. while Jordan, Davic, and Remy were in Moscow.

Rigo indeed had gone to D.C. and had attended a Redskins game, had lunch with the first lady in the White House, and had accompanied a Monuments tour with elementary-school kids.

But he stayed in the White House, in the bunker below the Oval Office.

Rigo had been told of the plot and had been disappointed: Russian President Makar Zubkov was called a loose cannon by the international media but Rigo thought he was just a no-nonsense leader. When the rest of the media had condemned Zubkov for firing his hunting rifle at an American "journalist" - truly just a muckraker for a tabloid - while he'd been out hunting, unaware he was being spied on by the journalist, Rigo had laughed and called Zubkov a man's man, unlike the rest of the world's leaders, none of whom could talk in any detail of sports.

"Why you bring this homosexual?" Zubkov asked Jordan as they shook hands, Davic right beside her, and Zubkov refused to shake his hand. He made it clear he was expecting Rigo, not Davic, to be the liaison between the two.

"Davic is my...right-hand man," Jordan said after awkwardly chuckling, afraid to use the word 'aide' now.

"Who knows what he does with it when he's alone," Zubkov said.

Davic wanted to harangue Zubkov over his country's anti-gay laws. He wanted to comment that it was a pity that among those who had starved to death under Stalin's regime, Zubkov's grandparents hadn't been among them - better for the world never to have known Zubkov at all - but he kept his mouth shut.

Zubkov wanted to take Jordan's people hunting, but after seeing Davic, the Russian president wanted him to stay behind in the Kremlin with Jordan.

"Mr. President, if the Prime Minister isn't going to be there, the only person able to speak on diplomatic matters is me," Davic said.

"We do not trust your kind with guns," Zubkov said.

"I am not a homosexual, Mr. President," Davic said measuredly. "And I know how to handle guns."

"How would you know?"

"I grew up hunting," Davic said. "I had a Remington 870."

"Is that what you called your vibrator."

"*No*. I killed a 12-point elk once, dressed it, and made dinner for my family."

Zubkov didn't immediately respond. Soon he scoffed.

They were not necessarily going hunting, but target shooting. In a field outside Moscow, paper animals had been nailed to trees, and Zubkov brought out a newly acquired Barrett .50-calibre sniper. He wanted to try it out with incendiary-tip rounds, and some of his security had brought fire extinguishers in case the rounds caused a fire to break out even on the snow-soaked trees.

Even though it was not hunting, the President and his security insisted Davic wear camo - fluorescent *pink* camo. Davic did not argue and put it on. He knew it was intended to embarrass and intimidate him and ultimately discourage him from the outing.

Zubkov fired off a few rounds, then stood back and invited Davic to try it out.

"Maybe it will remind you of what it was like to have a dick," the president said.

Davic fired two rounds, impressed by the gun's stability, power, and the explosion of the rounds. When he stood back from the gun, Zubkov motioned to one of his guards, who knelt beside the gun and wiped it down everywhere Davic's skin had touched it.

Davic rolled his eyes while Zubkov knelt once more and scanned for another target.

"What is Canada's position on the Kurds?" the Russian president asked.

Davic was relieved they were finally getting down to business.

"We are not getting involved in that part of the conflict. We will recognize them if they declare independence. Our neighbors to the south have a far more complex—"

"There is nothing complex about it. The Americans would rather negotiate with one leader than multiple states. Easier to infiltrate a country with only one leader."

"I'm not here to speak for the Americans. I know that Russia's actions in the Middle East and Eastern Europe are causing unrest for NATO members, and that's affecting Canada."

"The Americans love to concern themselves with things that don't have to do with them. Think they are the world's policeman."

"Your country is seen as unstable, intent on world domination."

"Crimea is ours, no matter what the Ukrainians say, it always has been. And the Ukraine is ours too, and they know that. Without Russia, the Ukraine would have fallen into some other hands. We've protected them and sustained them. And no, we do not want another US bastion in the Middle East."

"If Russia were to make some concessions, it would go a long way in showing that your country is a dedicated member of a global society intent on peace. You would get investment, support."

"What kind of concessions? You mean the climate-change scam."

"Well, the climate-change activists stopping Canadian oil production are certainly benefiting you; keeping us from becoming competitors on the world market," Davic said.

"And it was pushed by that Al Gore and because he is American, everyone bought into it. America has everyone in a chokehold now, and the UN penalizes countries who don't buy 'carbon credits.' Tell me what's so different between carbon credits and indulgences the Catholic Church sold. Nothing."

"If you will reduce your military presence in Syria, I will have our ambassadors talk with the Ukraine about Crimea."

"There is no need to talk, Mr. Woods. The Ukraine will perish without Russia and our resources, then Crimea will be ours without issue."

Pictures of Holodomor flashed through Davic's mind.

"If Russia allows the Ukraine to perish, the consequences from—"

"I don't care about the consequences from these groups, from *Canada*. If the US were not members of these groups and not so friendly with your country, you would cease to exist. Russia would not. Look at who Canada sent me to discuss these issues: faggot. Is it joke?

Even the American president is faggot. When Canada has *real* man running it, we will talk then. Until then, keep your proposals, Mr. Woods."

Zubkov called for the other guns he'd brought to be set up and for the contingent to move farther upland, where there were trees that hadn't been destroyed.

The current section of field was smoky and reeked of gunpowder and wet wood and smoke. Davic surveyed the scorched, exploded trees, soon replaced by living, untouched trees.

Zubkov's guards were all speaking in Russian to one another and none gave him a backward look as Davic's pace among them faltered, to the point that he fell out of the group. He watched them move ahead, their numbers vanishing over the snowy hill, and he was left behind.

Davic had been given his own bottle of vodka so he would not drink from the communal bottles. He knew he had to be seen drinking it, yet he feared what it would do to his behaviour and memory. He wandered down to the river and poured out most of the bottle, refilling it from the fast-moving frigid water. He scrambled back up the bank and took a deep swig of his vodka-flavored water and started back toward the group, expecting more ridicule.

Instead, the guns fired frantically and he heard screaming heading toward him. Davic froze and raised his single-shot rifle, scanning the upward slope ahead.

He saw Zubkov appear at the top of the slope, dashing downward, and behind him a bear giving chase.

As the two got closer to him, Davic fired at the animal, catching it in the shoulder.

"Hey!" Davic yelled and the animal paused to look at him.

Zubkov, still running, tripped and rolled down into a gully.

The bear changed targets. Davic fumbled to reload his rifle, stepping backward.

By now the security team had come down the slope and were dragging Makar to his feet. Makar watched as Davic leveled his rifle again just as the bear lurched at him. One of Zubkov's security officers aimed his own rifle and fired three shots into the bear's head and torso.

The bear was killed, its claw swipe slowing just enough for Davic to evade, and the animal slammed against a large dead tree, whose frozen trunk snapped and hit Davic on the head. He flew back into the river and was swept along by the strong current.

Zubkov screamed for his guards to go after Davic. The guards raced alongside the river until they came to a thick grouping of trees. They decided to head back to their car and drive to the other side of the river to look for Davic.

Once Davic recovered his wits, he managed to catch himself on the shore and pull himself on land. He took off the neon pink coat and tossed it back into the river. They likely knew he was a poor swimmer. When they found these articles – if they did – it may give them the impression he had drowned. It was time to make lemonade.

He took out his phone, thankfully in a waterproof case, pulled up the map of where they were: They had driven an hour and a half west of Moscow, to a portion of forest beside the Moskva River. 18 kilometers from Davic's current position was a town called Ruza and in looking up the town, he found it had several bars. He removed his phone's SIM card and turned off the location detection - which he did frequently for this job, every time reminding him of that day on the beach outside Sooke - and he used his phone's compass to guide him toward Ruza.

He was dressed in mostly water-resistant winter gear. His socks were soaked, as was his hair, but he jogged along the river to keep his temperature up. But even jogging, this trek in the snow could not help but remind him of the night his family had died, how he'd gone for help, walking along some rural, unlighted road in Ontario. Since then Davic had come to think of that as being the closest experience to Hell on earth as could be found. It was not torture, no fire or lava, just endless walking, repetition, exhaustion, freezing. He'd lived that night over and over so many times, including now. But he was in Ruza long before he'd been found by the snowplow driver that night - what had his name been? Buddy? Bud?

It was only mid-afternoon now, not late enough. In one of the bars, he got a glass of water and picked up an English Tolstoy from a bookcase and sat in a booth and read.

In a couple hours, he got some change from the bartender and called Jordan's phone number. She answered the unknown number with an agitated "Hello?"

"This is Davic. Answer only yes or no."

Jordan's silence voiced her surprise.

"Has the President returned to the Kremlin?"

"Yes," Jordan answered evenly.

"Are they trying to find me?"

"Yes."

"Are they worried?"

"Yes."

"Tell Potvin to call Richard back in Ottawa," Davic said. "He has contacts at *The New York Times* and BBC. Richard, in exchange for anonymity, tells them there is a rumor, unconfirmed by the Kremlin, that Prime Minister Jordan's Innis' aide Davic Woods has been kidnapped by the FSB, who may be interrogating him regarding his connection to President Delacroix's recent scandal. Yes?"

"Yes."

"Potvin then calls Rebecca," Davic said. "And she urges them to suspend the Russian ambassadors in Canada if I don't appear on camera within two days. Yes?"

"Yes."

"You text Delacroix *the truth*," Davic said. "You get him to talk to his people, who will remove the Russians if I don't turn up in two days. Yes?"

"Yes."

"If we need to get the British involved, I'll call you again from a different number."

"Yes."

Davic hung up. Then he looked around the bar and found a three-man group of elderly men, whom he approached and asked if they spoke English. They went silent when he introduced himself and all three nodded. Davic explained he was a sociology student from America researching differences in rural populations and city populations.

With his slim physique and babyface, Davic knew he was not physically intimidating and was naturally considered a non-threat. After explaining what he was doing here, the men started making jabs about him and welcomed him to their table to continue doing so.

After several more hours, during which Davic bought them as many rounds as they wanted, one of the men invited Davic back to his home to meet his wife and two teenage children, figuring he would want to get their takes for his research as well. Davic thanked him and followed him out to his truck.

The family, at first reserved, unsure of him, soon opened up and talked as easily as their non-proficiency in English allowed them. Davic slept on their couch in front of a fire and had breakfast with them the next morning.

By the next afternoon, he was in another Ruza bar with no TV. He called Jordan again.

"Has everything been done?"

"Yes."

"Is the President worried?"

"Yes."

"Do we need to involve the British?"

"No."

Davic hung up, then searched his phone's contacts for Zubkov's number and called it from the payphone.

"Mr. President," Davic greeted amiably. "Do I have your attention now?"

That night Zubkov, Jordan, and Davic worked out agreements that Zubkov would reduce military support in Syria and would cease encroachment upon Ukrainian territory. In exchange, Canada would offer members of its top tax brackets a deduction for investing in a future Russia-Canada resort in Crimea. To accomplish this, the Canadian ambassadors would talk with the Ukraine and Canada would openly support Russia's annexation of Crimea at NATO and the UN.

At the end of the meeting, just Davic was invited for dinner with the Russian President. "You're not gay. You just said that so you have leverage over Delacroix. He steps out of line, you go to the media and spin a sob story he can not disprove. Like I cannot disprove you were detained by intelligence. Blackmail."

Davic just grinned, letting Makar think whatever he wanted. He was happy to leave the President with the idea he was some manipulative political mastermind. It would at least make him think twice before messing with Jordan.

"I am impressed with your balls to pull that off. You have Delacroix's strings. There are a few issues I have with the US I would like to run past you first." Makar continued before laying out his issues with the US.

As Davic was leaving for the evening before he could be tempted with more drinks and woman, Makar pulled him aside as he put on his coat.

"Thanks for killing that bear, for that I owe you. I am having it made into a rug. I will have it shipped to you when it is done."

Before heading out on their flight back to Ottawa, Davic recorded a video on his phone, explaining he was fine, FSB had not been involved, he'd simply drunk too much vodka and gotten lost in the forest. He tweeted this and when he checked the news on his phone just before take-off, he saw the video was already being reported on, as was another story: Rigo had been photographed in a hotel room with first lady Queenie Delacroix. The photo had the two of them, as seen at an angle, perhaps from a tree, looking down through the open curtains of the window, standing nose to nose. The woman had Queenie's hair but only from a back view, and Rigo, though forward-facing, was blurry, his face partially obscured because he was kissing Queenie's lips.

The stories undoubtedly were reporting Rigo and the first lady were involved in a romantic affair, but all Davic cared about was what the stories reported the hotel as. In one, he saw the caption under the photo: *This photo allegedly shows the husband of Canada's Prime Minister Rigo Barbossa at the Dupont Circle with first lady Queenie Delacroix.*

Davic, from a pocket inside his jacket, removed the list of names he had composed with Jordan, Beau, and their heads of security. He found the Dupont beside Jordan's name and then the person whom Jordan had told Rigo would be staying at the Dupont during his D.C. trip.

He leaned in, showed the list to Jordan, and pointed at the name 'Alexandra Potvin.'

Looking behind her seat, Jordan saw Potvin in a window seat several rows back. She was chatting with a staffer, chuckling, unaware.

Chapter 16: Power Plays and Recriminations

The Canadians disembarked from the plane and headed into the hangar, Jordan, Davic, and Remy observing Potvin from three different angles.

The press were gathered outside the airstrip's fence, videoing and shooting pictures. Once hidden by the hangar walls, Remy flashed a signal to four of his men, who fell in line behind Potvin, following her as Remy led the procession out of the hangar and into the parking lot. Potvin was the first into one limo, at which point the PPS officers waved away the other staffers who tried to enter that limo. The four men entered and closed the door, then Remy went to the driver's door, pulled out the driver, and drove off.

Jordan and Davic watched the car get smaller and smaller, then Jordan led them to another limo while Davic started calling the Americans and the British.

The picture in the news was obviously photoshopped. The figure of Rigo was from an archive in the PR servers while the figure of Queenie was probably not Queenie at all. The trees and the window and the bedroom were high resolution, while the two figures were blurry.

Davic sent emails to the PR secretaries, giving them these details and instructing them to tell this to any reporters who called asking for comment. Beau told his PR staffers the same.

"This is just the tip of the iceberg," Jordan said in the limo.

"You have to see the tip to know it's there at all. We let Remy and the Mounties try to extract info from her. If needed, we call in the CIA. Get names, then prosecute -

attempted kidnapping, conspiracy to commit kidnapping, conspiracy to commit murder, treason. Find all the charges we can make stick."

Davic put his phone down, laid his head back, and thought: Once Potvin named who she was working for, the PMO could put out a name and motive to the press. Once this circulated a bit, it would give CSIS, the Americans, and the British another target, ease their suspicions that Davic and Jordan were operatives. With this legitimacy, CSIS would be more accommodating to Jordan.

Davic hadn't asked for his file since before Jordan got elected. To make such a request barely a year in office would arouse the suspicions of the intelligence community. Now was the time - ride the wake of confidence they were about to create, as well as get it when they could. Who knew when the next attack threatening Jordan's administration would come and how fast it would be before she was no longer in a position to get the file for him.

"Right before we started on your campaign," Davic began. "I asked you for a favor."

Jordan looked at him, remembering.

"Yeah, your CSIS file."

"After we disseminate the info Potvin will give us, I think would be a good time to ask for it."

Jordan smiled.

"I agree."

After a week, the Mounties had been unable to extract any actionable information from Potvin but CSIS turned in a report: There was a 85-percent match between the artist's rendering of the man posing as a diplomat's son and a mugshot for a man named Jacques Duchamp, whose father, Jérôme, had been imprisoned for 30 years for his involvement in the kidnapping of a Québec cabinet minister and a British diplomat in 1970. Called the "October Crisis," the kidnappings were committed by the Front de libération du Québec (FLQ), in order to gain more sovereignty for Québec.

Alexandra Potvin and Jacques Duchamp had attended the University of Québec at the same time and both were members of a Students for Socialism club for all four years.

Jordan's office relayed this information to the press, but was unwilling to confirm or deny that Potvin was in fact an FLQ operative. The Mounties put out a notice asking Duchamp to show up for questioning.

A week later Cy Drew came to Jordan's office at 24 Sussex.

"As requested," he said, putting down on the desk in front of her a manilla envelope with the label "Woods, Davic Hadrian James."

"Thank you," she said, setting it aside.

"Would you mind reading through it?" Cy asked.

As a matter of ethics, Jordan had intended to give it to Davic, then ask him what was in it. But Cy seemed insistent and being that he was Davic's foster father and probably knew what was in the file, Jordan opened the envelope.

Chapter 17: Blond Bacha Bazi

They had come into the village too fast, Davic thought, he hadn't had time to fully scan the area to ensure it was empty and free of IEDs. Despite this, they hadn't encountered any problems. But Davic made a mental note to be more assertive with Smyth before the next sweep. It wouldn't be easy – Smyth had no problem imposing his will on others. Davic admired his determination, but feared the danger such reckless abandon posed to all of the Marines. Davic would have to be strong with Smyth: The areas needed to be fully vetted before they entered. They couldn't always be this lucky.

The cool desert night air felt good on Davic's sunburnt face. He walked gingerly, still hurting from the sparring lessons the Marines had put him through. A sensor fell out of his arms and rolled against one of the abandoned houses of the village. He leaned down to pick it up.

"Hey, Boy it's past your bedtime," Rossco teased. "Finish up quickly and the Commander'll read you a bedtime story."

"I'll hurry," Davic replied with a smile. "I know you geriatrics need to get home to drink some prune juice before bed."

Davic wandered away from the group, searching for the other sensors. Smyth flashed Cook and Kenworth a signal to follow him as the rest of the team scouted this village. From the surveillance Davic had calculated the Butchers' hideout was nearby.

"How's he getting on with the others?" Smyth asked Rossco.

"They give and he gives right back," Rossco said. "Gonna need to learn how to retaliate from a practical joke."

"The sunburn?"

"Filled his sunscreen tube with mayo."

Smyth smiled.

"I still say he should be behind the lines," Rossco said.

"We just need to find the location of the Butchers. After that I'll send him back to HQ."

Smyth and Rossco stopped at the sound of trucks entering the village. Craning their necks, they saw three trucks pull into the town square - a flat area with a battered jungle gym.

Gunfire broke out before Smyth could signal the rest of his men, who dove for cover. The bullets were being fired in a flurry, like a drive-by, a wave of death.

Rossco and Smyth, from their crouch on one side of a house, saw Kenworth and Cook pull Davic into a line of buildings and disappear into one.

Smyth heard a gun cock in front of him and turning, the butt of a rifle knocked him out, as well as another for Rossco.

Kenworth and Cook pushed Davic up cement stairs, urging him to the next floor, but as he rounded onto one landing, he found himself blocked by three Afghani men, faces covered with bandanas, brandishing automatic rifles trained on Davic, Kenworth, and Cook.

Davic dropped the equipment in his hands, which he raised in submission. The Marines did as well, not trusting themselves to raise their guns and shoot before the Afghanis did, with Davic trapped in the crossfire.

The Afghanis barked at the three white men, who understood the gist: to turn around and head back down the stairs, and once out, the Afghanis pulled them to face the direction of the town square and kicked them forward.

The drivers of the trucks had laid down their guns and now were unloading barrel drums and Rubbermaid boxes, around which hovered a constant menagerie of flies.

Rossco and Smyth were pulled to the town square by the Afghanis who had captured the two Marines and bound their wrists and ankles. They hauled them by the ankles with rope like a fishing trawler hauls in netted fish.

Once all the containers had been unloaded, Smyth and Rossco were put in one bed, then Davic, Cook, and Kenworth were bound and put in a second truck. All their guns and knives were removed. The Afghanis then opened all the containers and removed the contents: Bloody meat, some decaying - black and green - other portions somewhat fresh.

The stench quickly made its way over to the conscious Marines, who winced and held their breath, for fear they would vomit.

The Afghanis used thick wire and large fishing hooks to hang the various meat pieces to the play structure. An Afghani took out a handful of the meat from a barrel drum and dropped it on the ground near the truck bed Davic was in. Squinting, he saw that among the tossed-out pile was a severed hand, violently hacked off the arm, and three fingers were missing, jagged bone stumps poking out of the flesh bases.

For a brief moment, Davic had the bizarre notion that the hand was from some kind of ape but the similarities to his own hands were too staggering to maintain this delusion.

From another barrel drum, one of the Afghanis lifted out a young boy, maybe six, who was in one piece, conscious but shivering with fear, eyes red from crying. He was naked and across his abdomen had been written:

خاين

The boy did not struggle in the least as two Afghanis carried him to the jungle gym and used leather strips to tie his wrists and ankles to the metal bars, so that he hung in between the stinking, rotted meat, the flies landing and crawling all over him. His mouth stayed tightly shut but Davic could hear whimpering from his throat.

One of the Afghanis removed a jerry can from one of the truck interiors and dumped petrol over the boy, the fetid meat, and the rest of the jungle gym.

"Oh my god," Davic groaned, quickly standing up in the bed. "No, don't—"

One of the Afghanis bashed his quadricep with the butt of his gun and Davic collapsed upon Kenworth and Cook, who were hypnotized, watching the Afghanis, standing in front of the jungle gym. Their leader stood in front of them, making a speech in Pashto and repeatedly pointing toward the Marines in the truck beds and the little boy, over his shoulder, crying, hanging limply.

Then the leader lit a match from a book.

"*Stop!*" Davic screamed, getting to his feet again.

The leader barked orders at two of his men, who then pulled Davic out of the truck bed and dragged him in front of the leader. The leader grabbed a handful of Davic's hair to keep his head up, then he threw the match onto the gas puddled on the cement below the jungle gym, and he peeled Davic's eyes open with his fingers, forcing the young man to watch everything.

The Butchers took the Marines to a building and secured them in separate prison cells, on either side of which was a corridor leading deeper into the building. With a combination of rope, chains, barbed wire, and the cell bars, the Marines were secured in stress positions.

Jaleel could tell just from looking at Davic that he was not military like the others. So Davic was left outside the line of cells containing his teammates, his wrists, ankles, and neck bound with chains and barbed wire, the neck chain hooked to one of the prison cell doors. Jaleel examined him in front of the other Marines: Aside from his skin tone, Davic looked like Jaleel's 16-year-old son. But this English - Canadian, British, American, they were all the same to Jaleel - was a commodity, with his pale complexion, blue eyes, blond hair.

Davic was as malleable as clay. Watching the child burn on the jungle gym had sapped his strength, his resistance. Jaleel wanted him to be able to observe the suffering of his fellows, to further drive home the consequences for his actions and what could happen if he reverted to his prior behavior of resistance.

Jaleel saw Davic's blue eyes wide with fear and felt the familiar arousal he always felt when he had total power of an enemy. This was slightly different, though, as never before had he captured such a prize as Davic.

Once his conquests were restrained, Jaleel knelt in front of Davic.

"You are a very beautiful thing," he told him in Pashto as he stroked the unblemished cheek.

It was clear Davic did not understand him. The blue eyes watered as they looked up. The child was terrified and sweet. His calloused thumb slid over Davic's soft quivering lips.

Davic pulled away when Jaleel petted his golden hair.

"Shy one, aren't you?" Jaleel said, hoping then that Davic understood Arabic but still no response. Jaleel detested speaking English but it was necessary for this. "Stillness."

Finally Davic understood.

"Please—" Davic started.

Jaleel slapped him.

"No speak if no speak. No manners?"

Davic allowed his captor to run his hand through his blond hair.

"Beauty sleep," Jaleel said and kissed the top of Davic's head and left.

Then they were alone.

"Roll call," Smyth said, stuck in the position of a wall sit with his hands held straight up.

"Rossco," Rossco called from his position of his arms around a block of wood behind his back, stuck in a crouch by chains around his waist connected to a hook in the floor.

The rest of the team announced their presence. They had all survived - unfortunately, Smyth thought.

"Did anyone get an idea for the layout?" he asked.

He and Rossco had been unconscious and Kenworth and Cook had been hooded when the Butchers had brought them into this torture chamber. Davic had been the only one with live eyes, but would he have paid any attention to how the building was laid out after what he'd seen?

"Cement and cinder blocks," Davic said mechanically. "No windows. Square. The cells are...10 by 10, metal-grate roof, walls welded rebar. The doors have padlocks."

"Know how to pick locks?" Rossco asked.

"Only digital ones. But I can try."

Davic twisted around as much as he could, feeling through the debris for some kind of long skinny tool to pick the lock securing the chains to his wrists and ankles. The barbed wire stabbed into his wrists and he remembered there was a major artery in the wrists. He thought suicide would be preferable to whatever the Butchers had in mind - Smyth and the Marines had never told him explicitly, only that they were brutal to their victims, the task force's informants, no doubt because they didn't want to scare Davic off the mission. But he couldn't leave the others here. Not being confined in one of those cages, he had the upper hand and best chance of finding a way to free the others. He could not give up.

It couldn't have been more than 15 minutes after Jaleel had left that footsteps once again approached their prison from the same corridor he had left by.

One of them was going to be taken away, Smyth thought, hoping it was not him. But then he berated himself for this slip in his military discipline: If it was not him, then it would be one of his men. Then he hoped it was him.

Once Jaleel appeared, Davic went as rigid as he had been when his captor had left.

"Ah, beautiful," Jaleel said, going over to Davic and raising his face.

Jaleel unlocked the chain tethering Davic's neck to one of the cell doors. With a hard yank, he pulled Davic across the floor.

"On feet!" Jaleel commanded.

Not having the use of his hands and unable to maneuver his feet, Davic struggled to even get into a crouch from which he could rise straight up. Then another yank on the chain that had connected his neck to a cell door pulled him to his feet.

"Leave him alone!" Smyth barked.

Jaleel grinned before putting a cattle prod between the bars of Smyth's cell to give him a shock. Smyth had no way to try to evade the shock, only take it, then his muscles went numb, the feeling gradually returning - and the first thing he felt was the stress his position was imposing on his muscles and bones.

Davic finally got to his feet, then Jaleel took the chain around his neck as Davic's lead and pulled him out of the prison chamber.

He led Davic into a tiled room like a high-school shower room from some '80s movie: shower heads on the walls at regular intervals, a drain in the middle of the graded floor.

On a stool Jaleel attached the chain from Davic's neck to a hook on the top of one wall. The stool wasn't high enough, otherwise Davic would have tried to knock Jaleel off and hope to break his neck.

There was a tap on one wall, to which Jaleel screwed on a hose and turned on the water. It was freezing, causing Davic to gasp when he was sprayed, feeling like glass slicing into his nerves. He was shivering when the hose was finally turned off. Jaleel tried to touch Davic but the boy pulled away, and Jaleel gave Davic a shock from the cattle prod.

The tiles were wet and slippery and Davic lost his footing but was held up by the chain around his neck. He could only catch small snaches of air and Jaleel watched in pleasure as Davic's face started turning blue, like his eyes. He unlatched the chain from Davic's neck and the boy flapped to the floor like a rag doll, and Jaleel listened to him sucking air.

"Behave, free hands," Jaleel said.

Davic nodded.

After his hands were freed, Davic propped himself against a wall and Jaleel rubbed soap over him. Jaleel wanted Davic perfectly clean to show him off. The bruises around the neck were a blemish on what was otherwise perfect porcelain skin. The bruises would be gone before he sold the boy. He was docile and it would not take much to get him trained. He only needed to learn a handful of Pashto commands.

Jaleel realized the boy was crying. He took Davic's chin and turned his face so he could see those blue eyes. He could see the the fear.

"You live, don't cry," Jaleel told him.

He would have beaten his own sons for crying but this one was unlikely to grow up to be a real man.

Jaleel hosed off the suds. The other chieftains would be jealous. They would ask where he got his new boy and make generous offers for a night of bacha bazi with him. He would wait to castrate him. He had enjoyed taking the aggression out of his boys.

He took Davic to another room. He watched the blue eyes look about with the realization of what this room was used for: There were wooden tables along the walls, on which were various tools that, in another time, were medical but were now rusted and bloodstained. Jaleel had seen that same fear in the eyes of all the other captives he'd brought in here. He enjoyed watching hope fade from the faces of the traitors. To see it vanish from the eyes of one of the infidels themselves was even more pleasurable.

Instead of taking his tools of torture to his porcelain doll, Jaleel took him to a stool in front of a table. Davic sat when prompted. Jaleel admired him like a great work of art. Davic was hunching his shoulders and cowering.

He took the boy's chin and started with the application of make-up. He had beautiful cheekbones and a wonderful face structure. Definitely blue eyeshadow.

When he was done, it was not his best work but would do for now. The other bachas could teach him better.

Jaleel then picked out clothing for Davic, rifling through a wooden box to pick out a pink dress. Davic fumbled pulling on the dress. Like most clothing, it was too wide and short for him. Davic had barely got the dress on himself when Jaleel pulled him into his body. His captor smiled at him, but Davic was a statue in his arms, eyes off to the side.

"Very beautiful," Jaleel said, pulling him in and giving Davic a kiss.

Davic pushed away and Jaleel grabbed a fistful of his hair to slam his head on the table, the makeup case rattling, lipstick and eyeshadow tubes rolling off.

"*No*," Jaleel said, waving a finger in Davic's face. This time Davic stayed still as Jaleel kissed him, first on his cheek, then trailing up to his neck, then down his spine.

Jaleel pressed his groin into Davic's back and Davic could feel an erection.

Jaleel slipped bells onto the barb wire around Davic's wrists, seeing then the barbs had extensively gouged his flesh. He regretted the scars this would leave, but figured he would just keep them covered until he was sold.

The bells rang from Davic's shaking, his eyes firmly

locked on the cement floor.

Jaleel completed the outfit with a coin-fringed sash tight around Davic's hips to cinch the oversized dress and accentuate Davic's slender figure.

"Dance," Jaleel said, pushing Davic into the open center of the room.

Davic was clueless.

"Dance!" bellowed Jaleel.

Davic sputtered helplessly, then started staggering about more than anything.

He fell. Jaleel walked over and extended a hand. As Davic reached for it, he was struck with the cattle prod, causing his body to convulse, wrists and ankles straining against the barbed wire, the pain of which he couldn't feel just then.

Jaleel picked Davic up, then slammed him face-down on another wooden table with leather strips laid out on it.

"Bacha bazi job: dance, funny." Jaleel growled

"What—"

Jaleel tossed Davic to the floor and pinned him with the cattle prod, shocking him till the battery ran out.

Smyth heard the men coming back to the cells, each step sending shocks of fear up his spine, convinced he would be next. He was the commander of this team and a colonel; they would use him for all the propaganda they could before he died from their torture, then leave him a mutilated corpse like so many of his informants - out on public display to serve as a warning.

Maybe that's what he deserved. To get the people of this region to cooperate and give him information, he had promised to free them from these warlords. At the time he had believed himself, but now he was angry at himself. After everything, he and his men had wound up the Butchers' prisoners, death all but certain, and if they died, then the families who had been tortured to death and the families that would be tortured to death will have been for nothing.

The Boy had stopped screaming finally. He was either dead or unconscious, and Smyth hoped the former. Listening to this Boy, who'd had no business being out in the field, who'd had no idea what he'd gotten himself involved in, scream and endure more pain than he'd ever experienced was hell for Smyth. The fact that Davic was here, getting the worst of the Butchers' punishment when he was the least deserving, when Davic was exactly the kind of boy that would fetch a high price among the warlords, who would use him to engage in their brutal sexual fantasies, made Smyth even angrier at himself. It was him who had made this happen. He knew he shouldn't have moved into the village so quickly, but he'd felt invincible.

His cell door was unlocked and one Butcher moved inside to release the chain suspending Smyth. He crumpled to the floor. His muscles were almost atrophied, rendering Smyth paralyzed. The Butchers picked him up, threw a hood over his head, and carried him off.

They brought him into the same chamber as Davic was in, wherein they hung Smyth on a ceiling hook by his barbed-wire handcuffs, burying the barbs in his flesh. Smyth could barely stand on the tips of his big toes.

He could hear a faint metallic clicking, like a bucket of coins on top of a washer. Two Butchers started whipping him with leather straps from one of the tables. He tried not to make a sound, lest his men hear their commander and lose hope - if they had any more to lose - but as the tails tore open his flesh, his will evaporated and he cried out.

That's what they wanted, he realized; they stopped whipping him after that.

He was barely conscious then, but heard Davic's voice weakly say his name, as distorted as one on land saying something to someone underwater.

The hood was removed. The place looked like a garage: cement-slab walls, benches of tools.

Smyth heard the metallic clinking again and saw Jaleel holding the cattle prod against pale flesh.

"Stand, bacha," the man said.

The trembling figure made the bells on his bindings ring as he stood. Smyth was horrified at how the Butchers had dressed him up, knowing all too well the reason.

The Boy was smacked across the back with a water hose.

"Leave him alone!" Smyth yelled.

In return the Butchers gave Smyth more lashings and cattle prodding. He could smell his own flesh and blood burning from the electric shocks.

Jaleel took a knife off a table and held it to Davic's neck. He grinned, watching Smyth's reaction. Davic, feeling the cool steel against his carotid artery, tried hard to be still but the bells kept jangling.

Jaleel sheared off the woman's garments, slowly savoring the reveal. Then he ran his hands over the Boy's bruised skin, cupping his flesh. Then he lowered the serrated knife, bending Davic's penis over the teeth.

Smyth was paralyzed, as though it were his own manhood being threatened.

After a moment, Jaleel removed the blade, leaving Davic intact. It would be enjoyable to watch Smyth suffer, but the warlords would pay Jaleel to be in the audience for the castration.

"You want me instead," Smyth said, on the verge of weeping.

In between crashing waves of despair, there was nausea.

Jaleel's comprehension of English was better than his speech.

"Ugly, old, you."

The Butcher wrapped his hand around Davic's neck,

then moved down to play with Davic's nipples.

"You goat fucker," Smyth groaned, pulling at his bonds, blood trickling down his arms.

Jaleel spoke to his underlings in the room, who hurried off but quickly returned with a stainless steel table, which they placed in front of Smyth, just out of reach.

Smyth could see the top of the table had been gouged, dried blood in the gashes.

Jaleel grabbed Davic by the chain around his neck and pulled tight so he could hear the Boy fight to breathe. Davic's thin hands pulled at the chain, fighting for enough slack so he would not pass out. Then Jaleel pulled Davic around the table so he and Smyth were looking across it at each other. Davic's eyes were bulging, pleading for help.

Then Jaleel eased up his hold on the chain, allowing Davic to suck in a gasp, before the Butcher slammed the side of his head upon the metal table. Once Davic was dazed, Jaleel gave orders to the other Butchers, who quickly tied Davic's arms and legs to the table's legs.

A jar of some kind of white jelly was dumped on the table, next to Davic's head, the sound of which made his eyes snap open.

Jaleel, behind Davic, ran his hand over Davic's butt. Smyth saw the realization hit the Boy of what Jaleel was intending to do. Davic's eyes opened wide as he tried to look at his captor.

"No, please—" Davic started but Jaleel slapped him, smashed his head into the metal table again, and one of the other Butchers zapped him with the cattle prod.

Davic managed to make eye contact with Smyth. Smyth knew The Boy was looking for help or some reassurance. Smyth wanted nothing more than to kill the Butchers and save Davic from what was going to happen.

"Woods, just go somewhere else in your head, someplace happy for you," was all he could offer.

Davic closed his eyes and nodded slightly as tears

rolled down his cheeks. Smyth let out an audible sob and turned his eyes away. He had failed the Boy in the worst way possible.

Davic screamed when they took him, limbs trying to flail in struggle but the ropes were too tight, so all he accomplished was tearing his flesh against the barbed wire. Jaleel hit the blond boy over the head with his elbow, incapacitating him.

Once he was done, Jaleel was thinking about keeping this one. He motioned for the other two Butchers to have their reward as well. As they both began, Jaleel went to Smyth, who had closed his eyes and put his head down as far as he could. The Butcher kneed him in the testicles, then jerked his head up.

"You, seat row front," the Butcher said, teasing the colonel's crying.

Davic was conscious but was motionless, just waiting for it to end. If he struggled, they may kill him, but if he were compliant, he may live yet and apparently thought there was chance enough for life outside this building to do so.

Smyth, on the other hand, was pessimistic: Had the Boy ever been intimate with someone, hopefully someone he loved? How this could not shatter his life beyond repair was beyond belief.

Smyth and the others were not valued by the Butchers and other warlords as Davic was. The Marines' pain and suffering had an end date, and there was comfort in that.

But Davic was a commodity and his owners would try to keep him alive by any means necessary. He was destined for a life of suffering and torment.

The coward in Smyth also took comfort in the fact that he would be dead and would not have to reveal to Cy and Lemma that their foster son, their computing genius, had endured suffering because of his actions.

Once the other two were done, Jaleel lifted up Smyth's head and he saw in the Butcher's hand some blue pills. Smyth snapped his mouth shut as Jaleel tried to throw the pills down his throat but when he could not get Smyth to open his mouth, Jaleel had one of his fellow Butchers hold Smyth's nostrils shut.

It was only a matter of time until Smyth had to open his mouth for breath, at which point Jaleel threw in the pills and held his hand over Smyth's mouth until he swallowed.

Then Jaleel and another Butcher unhooked Smyth and pulled him behind Davic, and Smyth's body convulsed with silent weeping. His body soon betrayed him, the filthy hands of the Butchers jerking him.

Blood was spilling down Davic's legs and they were bloody scratch marks in his back and sides. He was too still. When Smyth was stiff but did not move in, the Butchers tried to push him forward, but he dropped himself onto the floor and let them beat him, yelling at him to take what was his. When the Butchers tried to haul him to his feet, Smyth pulled himself back down, at which point they beat him more.

Disappointed, Jaleel ordered Smyth be put back in his cell. He wanted to get some sleep before they started working on the videos - breaking bones, cutting appendages, then limbs, organs, peeling nails - for the West.

Jaleel first felt for a pulse and found it in Davic's neck. His eyes were open and responded to light but did not track movement. The Butcher got Davic cleaned up, then carried him into his own sleeping quarters, just on the other side of this room. It would be nice to have a warm body in bed with him. He could tell the Boy was broken, as impotent as a newborn. Falling asleep, Jaleel contemplated keeping the Boy, chopping him up and making his comrades - Western dogs - eat him on camera.

Chapter 18: Scythe No More

Davic came back to some kind of consciousness and found himself on a bed of grimey yoga mats, old clothes for pillows. It was cold in the cement-walled room. Above him, Davic saw his father, a hand on his son's shoulder.

"It's too cold, Dav," James said.

Davic looked up in disbelief. He expected his father to vanish between blinking his eyes, but James was still there when his lids reopened.

"Are you really here?" Davic asked, his voice high and weak.

"Yes, I am."

Davic thought this must be a dream. A few times in his life, he'd been able to reason, even while asleep, that something he was dreaming was indeed a dream. But he didn't care, he hoped he'd never wake up. He felt no pain, though he knew he should from something that had happened but he couldn't remember what. He couldn't remember where he was or what he did when he wasn't dreaming. All he could remember was that when he was dreaming, his father wasn't there and that made him sad and all he wanted was for his father to be with him and he was here now, so the dreaming was all that mattered.

"You've sure grown up. I think you're taller than me," James said, a proud smile on his face.

"When the dementia really set in, Grandma thought I was you," Davic replied.

"You've done very well, son," James said. "I'm proud of you."

Davic smiled, he could feel his sleeping body's eyes getting wet even as his dreaming eyes did.

"You don't know how much that means to me," Davic said.

"But this isn't the end," James said. "You have a lot more to do."

James pointed at the ground beside Davic's head and when he looked, Davic saw a screwdriver sticking out of a pile of clothes - he had no idea whose they were or how long they'd been there.

"You may be too young to remember, but I remember when you figured out how screwdrivers worked," James said. "I had a meeting on the phone and you were playing by yourself. I was an hour and a bit. I came out and you had taken off every electrical plate cover and several cupboard doors in the kitchen. You were so proud of yourself, I couldn't get mad at you."

"I remember Mom yelling at me."

"She still loved you."

"When she was sober," Davic added.

James reluctantly nodded

"Tools can be used for both creation and destruction," James said. "It depends on intent. I think there are some things around here that need your expert craftsmanship."

James then pointed to the other side of Davic's head, and looking over his shoulder, Davic found a block of wood with a screw sticking out of its hole. He picked up the screwdriver and inserted it into the head of the screw, but when he tried to twist it down, the screw sank straight back into its hole.

Jaleel had left and another Butcher had taken his place, to guard Davic, but he had drifted asleep. He jerked awake when Davic rammed the screwdriver into the side of his neck and kept twisting. The Butcher couldn't fight back. Davic continued prodding the hole after the body had stopped twitching.

"That's a deep counterbore. Is there a cap to plug it?" Davic commented as he finally took his screwdriver out of the hole.

Davic turned to his father to see if he had done what needed to be done, and James nodded.

"Don't worry about it, there's more," James said. "Go in the next room, there are more tools."

Davic, naked, stood and went into the next room, where there were tables of tools, both industrial and medical, all of which looked medieval. He found a leather toolbelt and put it on, then filled it with a hammer, another screwdriver, a chisel, and a hatchet.

"I think those'll do the job," James said. "You ready?"

"Just one question. Why did you name me Davic?"

James grinned, as though remembering a long-forgotten and embarrassing drunken night.

"I'd like to tell you it's a combination of David and Victor, but the truth is I was so over the moon when you were born, I forgot the last line in 'd' at the end of 'David' on your birth certificate." James paused, looking into his son's eyes. "We could have fixed it, but I figured there's no one like you, so you should have an original name."

Davic smiled as James led him to a hallway, then to a room that had several empty prison cells.

"I'm stuck, I need your help, OK?" James said.

Davic nodded.

"I need you go get the keys to unlock those cages," James said, his face going paler than usual and ice forming in his blond hair and eyebrows.

He pointed to a thick wooden board, a nail standing on its tip upon it, and a rusted shovel lying beside the board.

Davic first went to the wooden board and hammered in the nail with three strikes.

The Butcher managed to react to the first strike and scream but the final two blows cracked his skull open and brain matter oozed out onto the floor.

Smyth and the others in their cages, in stupors from

the their constant torturous positions, were stirred back into consciousness.

Then Davic took out the chisel and hammered its top to drive its tip against the rust on the shovelhead, peeling away the oxidation.

Hammering the chisel cracked open the second Butcher's chest, penetrating his heart. The Butcher didn't even have a chance to scream.

Davic cleaned two strips from the shovel, then James told him that was enough.

"Behind you," James said.

Davic turned and saw a large fire-ravaged tree had grown up through the cement floor, then burst through the ceiling, right behind him. He took out his hatchet and hacked at the dead limbs, looking at his father to know when to stop. He smashed the hatchet into the trunk a few times, then James told him that was enough.

A man lay on the floor screaming in agony, his arms severed beside him. Blood pumped from his stumps, the volume dying until the bleeding stopped altogether.

"Get behind there," James said, pointing to a metal box a foot away from a wall. When Davic crouched behind it, a door on the wall across from it appeared, open, and torrential rain flew in at an angle. It poured for several seconds, then stopped.

Gunmen stormed into the room, firing without looking. The bullets bounced off the cages the Marines were locked in, igniting cascades of sparks. Somehow none struck the trapped men.

A ceasefire was called with the realization the room

appeared empty.

Smyth and his men could see Davic behind the box and held their breath.

Still huddling behind the box, Davic looked above him and saw the roof had rematerialized and from it hung a bare light bulb, shining. He got the hammer from his toolbelt and hurled it up, shattering the bulb.

When he stood, he saw, in moonlight coming in through the open door, three other scorched trees were in the room. Davic went to the door, closed it, then used the hatchet to hack at the trees, sensing where they were in the darkness. As he was swinging, the roof vanished and the rain returned, pouring, saturating Davic, but his grip on the hatchet was strong.

The bullets flew about the dark room. The noise of the echoing gunfire deafened the Butchers, making them easy prey for Davic's hatchet. Their blood made the floor slick.

Finally the rain stopped.

"Get behind the door," he heard James say in the dark.

Davic found the door, then stood against the wall beside the closed door. It opened, concealing him, and more dead trees replaced the trees Davic had destroyed. Davic hacked at these, but more grew spontaneously. James stopped Davic's hacking frenzy and told him to go down the corridor behind him. Davic spun on his heel and hurried away from the trees as the rain started pouring on him again.

The Butchers were stunned: Either their wild gunfire was completely missing the blond bacha or else he was impervious to pain.

The rain stopped when Davic reached the end of the

corridor, in a rectangular room with a long nailboard, hanging from which were rings of keys.

"You need the padlock keys," James said and Davic saw his father with his security blanket from childhood over his shoulders, ice forming on his cheeks. "The keys are small and look the same."

Davic found a ring larger than the others but whose dull-gold rings were small and identical. He put them in a pocket on his toolbelt.

Turning back, he saw three wooden beams, such as are used to support the porch roof of a house, lined the corridor he needed to take to get back to the prison room. Each of these beams had a string of Christmas lights hanging from their tops.

The rain started again but Davic found a staple gun on the table perpendicular to the nailboard and he used this to staple the strings of lights to the beams. He put four staples in one beam, five in the next, and three in the third, and the rain stopped.

The bacha had found a loaded gun left sitting on the table. The three Butchers fell dead, torn apart by the bullets, their guns clattering across the floor. Davic rushed over their bodies, muttering something about how the Christmas lights were tangled.

Once in the prison room again, Davic pulled the keys out of his belt and selected one of the dozen at random, to try to unlock one of the cages.

He heard metal smacking metal, descending, then a heavy pipe smashed the back of his head and Davic fell onto his hands and knees, blood streaming down his neck and forehead, into his eyes.

Glancing behind him, Davic saw a new dead tree had formed.

Then he looked over at his father. He was writing on

the back of the unframed family Christmas picture. He was dying, Davic knew. He had to hurry!

A bullet had struck Jaleel but hadn't hit anything vital. When he'd hit Davic with the metal pipe, there was a cracking of bone, which gave the last of the Butchers a smile. It didn't look like Davic was dead yet, but it was just a matter of another strike of the pipe. Then the bacha's comrades would suffer even more than Jaleel had planned.

Davic pulled out the hatchet again, swung it over one shoulder into the tree's trunk, then stabbed the screwdriver beside the embedded hatchet. He was dizzy but he got back to his feet, tearing out the hatchet.

Another pipe hit his head, staggering him but he remained upright, and swung the hatchet again.

Jaleel collapsed, blood pouring out of his mouth, his chest, and his stomach, in which the hatchet remained lodged. All the bullets in the bacha – how could he have been bested by this thin, lanky, terrified boy? The only satisfaction he could find was that they would both soon die and the other Westerners would starve and rot in here.

Davic looked over at his father, stoically standing in a corner.

"Hold on, I'll get you out!" Davic cried.

He retrieved the keys from the ground and unlocked the first prison cell and when he staggered in, he saw the car crash: His father wedged in his seat because of the crumpled driver's door, his mother dead in the passenger seat, and just the tip of Evelyn's car seat sticking up above the driver's seat headrest.

James' hand, sticking out the broken window, limply waved Davic over and Davic approached, crying. James' hand opened for Davic to drop the keys and when he did, James looked up at Davic again, the tears frozen on his face.

"You have to keep going," James said.

Smyth, his chains unlocked, painfully pulled his limbs out of the barbed wire and ropes, then caught Davic as the Boy collapsed.

He was riddled with bullet wounds, flesh torn, his head gushing blood. He had just witnessed the Boy take a beating that would have killed any Marine.

Smyth hated to lay Davic down but he had to free the others, the first of which was Rossco, whose numb limbs made him crawl into Smyth's cell to examine Davic, the head wound vicious, painfully clear. The skull was visible through the wound and was fractured. Rossco opened Davic's eyes and waved his hand in front of them, but there was no response. Davic had lost consciousness and Rossco couldn't imagine he would regain it.

Once the others were freed, the Marines carried Davic out of the building, the mangled bodies of the Butchers strewn all around, their blood on the walls. Kenworth hotwired a pick-up truck. Rossco and Smyth braced Davic in the bed against the jolts of the truck driving across desert in search of a road.

Chapter 19: Circular File

Jordan closed the file and held her face and cried silently for a minute.

Cy was also tearing up, knowing what was within the file.

"I brought you his file because you are my boss, and I'm required by law to do so," he said. "But I beg you not to share it with him. Most people have the misfortune of remembering the worst things that have happened to them. Thankfully, Davic isn't one of them."

Jordan struggled with it all that day. Since she had known him, he'd always been preoccupied with gaining access to this file, and Jordan was not ignorant that this was probably the primary reason he'd wanted her to run for Prime Minister. That had been OK with her, at least she knew what it was he wanted and how to ensure loyalty, and the drive he'd exhibited in order to get her in position to get his file had reaped plenty of benefits for her too.

Would she have worked with him if she'd known from the start what was in his file?

He had tried to kill himself just before she'd met him, she had rescued him, and if Jordan had known what the file contained, she would have taken him straight to the hospital.

In looking over the file some more, she saw Davic had gone to a rehab in Victoria following his hospitalization.

She thought back on that day at the beach: Davic had told her he'd tried to kill himself after his proposal to a girlfriend had been rejected. Jordan had always been suspicious, but the simple story was solid and Davic seemed stable, particularly after they'd slept together.

God, what had she done? Davic had wanted to kill

himself, probably because CSIS had released him, and then they'd had sex. What had that done to Davic's state of mind?

Had she enslaved him? Beneath his dedication to getting her the power to get this file, was there some underlying brainwashing? That would explain why Davic had never, until Nigella, shown an interest, least of all romantic, in any woman - or person, for that matter.

Was he in love with her, obsessed with her? They were surely in love. They had worked closely for the past four years and Davic knew everything about Jordan and Jordan had thought until now that she'd known almost everything about Davic. But she didn't.

And maybe that wasn't his fault. She didn't know how his 'retrograde amnesia' affected his memory. He remembered his childhood and most of his time in CSIS, but she didn't know when his memory started again after that.

Did he remember they had had sex? Did he remember attempting suicide? God, what if his memory hadn't worked for her entire campaign? Could he have run on autopilot, working to get her elected?

If that was the case, Jordan could not bear the thought she had used him as some kind of Manchurian problem-solver.

Jordan knew, after what she had read, she could not look at Davic the same way. She wished she could unread the file, but the words, the images were etched on her mind and she would be reminded every time she saw him of what pain humans could inflict on each other. He was fragile and vulnerable and she had taken advantage of him. Guilt overwheled her. She knew she could not make up for the past but with the knowledge came the responsibility to protect Davic.

Jordan regretted telling Davic she had requested his file. He'd been dropping in every day since to see if it had arrived.

Today when he came in, Jordan was crying, her chair turned away from her desk. He crouched beside her and put an arm around her, asking what was wrong. Jordan chewed her fingernails for a moment.

"Do you remember how we met?"

Davic was struck off guard by this question.

"Yeah, it was on the beach."

"Do you remember what happened? Why you were there?"

"Yeah…"

"What?"

"I was...My girlfriend rejected my proposal."

Jordan cringed, looking into his eyes, searching for some flutter, some tell. But she knew he was a master manipulator and had benefited from that quality.

"You're *lying*," Jordan said.

"How?"

"There was no girlfriend."

"What makes you think that?"

Jordan only stared at him.

"*What* makes you think that?"

"I saw your file."

His whole body seized up. His brain was lit on fire and a tsunami of fear rushed up his spine, creating a confusing mix of emotion. He snapped his head all around, searching the immediate area.

"I gave it back to CSIS," Jordan said.

Davic felt a sledgehammer hit him in the gut. His goal had slipped through his fingers.

"Why would you—" he jolted upright, standing over Jordan. "What did it *say*?"

"It said you were in a rehab center in Victoria."

"I *know* that—"

"*I* didn't—"

"Why was I there?"

"Why didn't you tell me the truth?"

"*Why was I there?*"

"It didn't say—"

"You're *fucking lying!*"

Davic slapped her desktop to the floor, shattering it, and Jordan stood out of her chair and moved away from Davic.

"Dav—"

"What did it say?"

"It...a computer fell on your head at CSIS."

"*Why* would that be *sealed*? *Stop lying to me!*"

He smashed his fist upon the top of Jordan's desk, making the Prime Minister flinch.

"Davic—"

"The only reason you're in the position to keep this from me is because of *me*," Davic said, tears pouring down from his eyes, lips quivering, his face twisting.

"I'm not doing this to be malicious—"

"I have only ever asked you for *one thing*. I have done *everything* to make sure you got where you wanted to be when *you* had no fucking idea how to get there! I keep you and your fucking mongrel husband in line so these people don't throw you out *on your ass!*"

He smashed the desk again.

"And in return you fucking lie to me, you dangle my file in front of me, then snatch it away, *why*? Am I a fucking rabbit to you? You fucking ungrateful *bitch!*"

When he smashed the desk a third time, he broke through the wood top, and Jordan let out a scream. She saw Davic's clenched fist, squeezed tight, white as a snow, shaking, torn skin bleeding.

"Get out of here, Davic," Jordan said stiffly, afraid to move in the slightest.

Davic's eyes were crying but his emotions were so disoriented, he didn't know whether to cry or maul Jordan.

He hurried out of Jordan's office, opening the door and pushing through the crowd of staffers who had gathered out in the hallway.

After a few days, Jordan hoped Davic had cooled down enough and called him.

"I love you, Dav, and you have to believe me when I say I want the best for you. If I thought seeing your file would be in any way beneficial for you, I would show it to you."

Davic was quiet. Jordan had been afraid, after he'd left her office the other day, that Davic would hurt himself. She had Remy visit him every day since and the PPS captain had returned reports that Davic seemed depressed but otherwise safe.

"I want you to come back," Jordan said.

"I can't."

"Why?"

Davic couldn't articulate it. The silence over the line made Jordan's heart throb.

"When you were trying to convince me to run for Prime Minister, you told me you quit CSIS because they demoted you. Of course the truth was CSIS released you. But you wanted to kill yourself because of it, because you couldn't do what you felt you were meant to do anymore. Was that true?"

"Yes."

"You helped me become Prime Minister because you thought I could help people. But I can't keep helping people without you. Isn't that a better reason to live?"

"I can't stand not knowing...that you know and won't tell me."

"Maybe because up until this point, it's all that you've had. But if you get yourself out of your tunnel vision, I think you'll see there's more in your life: You are a great man and friend. You can accomplish anything you set your mind to. And what about Nigella?"

"What about her?"

"Do you love her?"

"I...She doesn't know - she can't know."

"If you care about her, then it's worth the risk. Fuck what Basil wants. You have to try. If she can't handle the truth about you, that's one thing. But you have to give her the option. She's a grown woman, you don't need to make decisions for her."

Davic was quiet, thinking.

Jordan was not sure things between them could go back to normal. But maybe they just needed time. If she could keep him at 24 Sussex, maybe they could figure out how to make this work.

"Come back, be Rigo's assistant for a little while," Jordan said. "If you hate it and want to leave, fine."

"*When* I hate it...can I go back with you?"

Jordan chuckled.

"Of course."

After hanging up, Davic stared at Nigella's phone number on his phone screen for 10 minutes, weighing the pros and cons. Could he tell her the truth, violate the pact he and Basil had made not to involve her in his work? With the perpetrators of the events in Toronto still mostly unknown, how could he expose her to the danger, risk getting her kidnapped or killed?

But he remembered what Jordan had said: That would be a decision only Nigella could make.

He called her.

Chapter 20: Hospitable Arrangements

In the ICU room, Davic was in another coma. How many people live to be in two comas in their life? Even fewer would survive both ordeals, Cy thought.

Smyth had just come in, carrying a bag from which he pulled out the framed photo of Davic's family. Cy set it on the dresser next to Davic's bed, the heart monitor beeping steadily on the other side, the IV dripping, the ventilator rasping as it pumped air in and out of Davic's lungs.

"The press is calling him the 'Hero of Hull,'" Smyth said.

Cy said nothing in response.

Davic had already been through two rounds of surgery to extract the bullets he'd taken when he and Rigo had been ambushed on the café terrace. In addition, he was receiving regular transfusions and fighting a heart infection caused by sepsis from a perforated bowel. He was on a heavy regiment of antibiotics to prevent septic shock from setting in, but so far the medicine hadn't proven effective. And as if that weren't enough, the infection was causing swelling around his heart and pushing toward congestive heart failure. The doctor had put Davic's name on a heart-transplant list, though if the infection couldn't be stopped, a new heart wouldn't matter.

Cy put a hand on Davic's forehead: He was burning up, the hair plastered with sweat to his forehead and temples.

The doctor, by asking, had reminded Cy he was Davic's power-of-attorney, as he'd been when Davic had been hospitalized after Afghanistan.

"What's the long-term prognosis if he survives?" Cy had asked the doctor.

"Depends on how much organ damage the infections cause. It's currently centering around his heart. It would be months, if not years of physical therapy, still with lifelong impairments."

"Rossco's on his way," Smyth said to Cy, who had requested and authorized the Marine doctor to access Davic's medical reports.

In a few moments, Smyth's phone rang. He only answered it after looking at the screen: Bowser.

"Parking garage. Bring Cy," was all he said.

The Mounties had been interrogating Potvin for a week but had relayed no new information regarding Jacques Duchamp.

The one culprit of the ambush at the café, whom Davic had incapacitated and the Mounties had arrested, had been given to CIA agents, who'd flown to Canada on Delacroix's and Bowser's orders to interrogate the suspect.

Under any other circumstance, Cy would not have left Davic's side. But Bowser would only call now if he had information critical to finding the terrorists. He followed Smyth into the parking garage, going through the empty waiting room.

Beside Bowser's black Cadillac SUV, Delacroix's chief of security handed Cy the café shooter's mugshot:

"Alex Brown, goes by Alexandre Bignon. Some Antifa guy, hellbent on overthrowing the patriarchy and capitalism. He's part of the Neo-FLQ. Implicated Potvin and this guy," Bowser handed Smyth another picture of a man on a crowded street but clearly the subject. "Recognize him?"

"Vaguely."

"Gilbert Plonk. The journalist. Said he was one of the other gunmen."

"Did he say who the third was?"

"Guy named Pierre Dembélé. He's one of LaSalle's top aides."

"Jesus," Smyth muttered.

"Is LaSalle…?"

"We're trying to determine that. Potvin and this *Bignon* guy haven't confirmed it. We're gonna...ask Plonk and Dembélé."

"Be discreet," Smyth said.

Bowser scowled at the superfluous reminder.

Smyth and Cy headed back to Davic's room.

Once back on the ICU floor, both men heard commotion coming from Davic's room at the end of the hall.

The room was filled with nurses talking over each other, the machines beside the bed blaring their alarms. Both Smyth and Cy watched solemnly.

But then the alarms went off, and the crazed nurses gathered calmed down, a palpable sense of relief among them. The machines were beeping rhythmically again.

One nurse turned and saw the two men outside the doorway.

"Somehow...he must have torn out his IV," she said. "I'm sorry, he's stable again."

Once the nurses were gone, Cy sat beside Davic's bedside again, holding his hand and struggling not to cry. Smyth had to leave, making an excuse that he needed to coordinate RCMP cooperation with the CIA in their search for Plonk and Dembélé.

Cy hated himself for leaving Davic's side. Any moment could be his last. He hoped there was enough warning before Davic died that he could call in Jordan and Nigella and let them say goodbye. He cried harder. Would Lemma want to bring in a priest to say last rites? Or some other clergy? Davic was not religious but it would help those that would be left behind.

Once his crying abated a little, Cy looked at the photo

Smyth had brought: the Christmas picture. Then underneath the framed photo, he found a second loose photo, edges frayed, the picture itself folded and aged.

When Cy picked it up, he recognized Davic and James in it: Davic couldn't have been older than four here, sitting beside his father on James' workbench, holding screwdrivers crossed like light lightsabers, both smiling, Davic's joy infectious.

The picture could only have been taken by a third person or maybe timed on a tripod.

Remembering James had a habit of writing on the backs of photos, Cy turned the loose picture over and found, written in ink untouched by the forces that had aged the rest of the photo, was a message:

"I'll see you when you get better.
Love, your Uncle."

About the Author

Melissa Hailey has been involved in politics from a young age. She grew up in Dubai and was able to see the world as a child. After dinner she would discuss and debate her father on a wide variety of topics and at 22, she was first elected to office, becoming the youngest female elected in Canada. She served two terms as a municipal councilor. The perpetual policy wonk (political nerd), she has never been a fan of the political dramas distracting from the issues at hand. She is now turning the political head games and emotional manipulation into plot lines.

An entrepreneur, she has owned and operated a kayak-tour company for a decade. You can find her on the farm with her chickens and mini horses. She lives in British Columbia and enjoys taking her nephew out in the horse cart for picnics.

CPSIA information can be obtained
at www.ICGtesting.com
Printed in the USA
LVHW112335220419
615173LV00001B/16/P